Catherine Terrick lives in Sudbury, Ontario, Canada with her husband of 47 years, Michael. Her love of writing began at an early age, entering a local writing contest, she won 1st prize and *Blinky, The Christmas Elf* was featured on the front page of the Northern Life Newspaper, complete with a picture she had drawn of Blinky. She spends her summers on beautiful Manitoulin Island, which she calls her 'happy place' and does much of her writing there. This is her first published work. She is currently working on the final chapter in the *Two 'fer* series titled *Down the Rabbit Hole*.

In Memoriam

I'd like to dedicate this book to members of my family who have left us too soon.

Joe, Roy, Dominic, Billy, John-Boy, Wayne, Seany-Boy

And Especially Our Dear Jesse

Forever in our hearts.

Catherine Anne Terrick

TWO'FER

AUSTIN MACAULEY PUBLISHERS™

LONDON • CAMBRIDGE • NEW YORK • SHARJAH

Ordering Information
Quantity sales: Special discounts are available on quantity purchases by corporations, associations, and others. For details, contact the publisher at the address below.

Publisher's Cataloging-in-Publication data
Terrick, Catherine Anne
Two'fer

ISBN 9781649796011 (Paperback)
ISBN 9781649796004 (Hardback)
ISBN 9781649796028 (ePub e-book)

Library of Congress Control Number: 2022905312

www.austinmacauley.com/us

First Published 2022
Austin Macauley Publishers LLC
40 Wall Street, 33rd Floor, Suite 3302
New York, NY 10005
USA

mail-usa@austinmacauley.com
+1 (646) 5125767

Many thanks to my personal human thesaurus and my spell-checker, my hubby – M.T.G.

Specially to my husband of 47 years – my chief cook and bottle washer who makes me laugh every day. Love you, Mikey.

Chapter 1

"No, I'm finished—I'm not going back."

"Come on, Noah, you know it was just another fight."

"No, this was different—the bastard came after me this time and Ma tried to stop him. He beat her so bad I thought she was dead. He's never beat her like that before. If he's coming after me now and Ma keeps trying to protect me, it'll just be a matter of time until he does kill her. I have to go, besides, I almost killed him myself tonight—maybe I should go back and finish the job."

"He's got a mean streak a mile long, Noah…he's beaten men twice your size before. Unless the sod has passed out—no puny little 14-year-old would have a chance at that."

"Well, I've got to do something—she's my Ma and he will kill her one day, Kaleb…he will. Maybe if I can find work I can save up enough money to get her out of there, away from the old bastard once and for all. I have to find work somehow, Kaleb, I just have to."

"Well, there's nothing around here, Noah. I know cause I've been looking. Ever since my Dad died, it's been up to me to put food on the table but it's getting harder and harder. Being the oldest with five others at home—Mum can't provide for us…there's barely enough for us to eat. It breaks my heart to see the little ones cry from hunger."

"There's just no jobs to be had here."

"Let's just go then, Kaleb—get the hell out of here."

"Where would we go, we've never even been to town?"

"They're always looking for good men on the fishing boats, aren't they?"

"Good men!" He laughed. "You're 14 years old—who's going to hire you?"

"I don't look 14," he said huffily, "and you are 17, nearly grown—if they're hard-up for help, they won't look that close."

Looking out across the fields, the stillness of the night envelops them. They each contemplate what they are about to do. The night air was bitter, colder than usual for that time of year.

Kaleb looked down at the thin clothes they were wearing and realized they had no money, no provisions…they'd never even been away from home before…nothing to start out with on such a momentous journey. Kaleb knew this decision was going to change their lives forever and the enormity of what they were about to do was overwhelming. He felt anxious and full of doubt. Noah too, was scared but he'd never admit it. He'd always looked at Kaleb as a big brother and would never want to disappoint him, so he would continue with his false bravado.

As Kaleb continue to weigh the pros and cons he realized that Noah's situation at home had become so violent, that he would not have been surprised if someone was killed in the near future. It was only heading one way…and that was to murder, no doubt.

His problem was completely different, but just as critical. Since his Dad had passed he had scrambled to put food on the table for his family…but there just weren't any jobs in their little farming community. His Mum scratched by selling a few eggs from their hen. She also took in laundry for a few of the grander ladies in the small town…but even that was petering out.

"Come on Kaleb…Let's just go. We got nothing holding us back," Noah pleaded. It seemed like a no-win situation to Kaleb. If they stayed—nothing good would come of that. But if they went, and one or both of them didn't make it back…that would seal both families' fate.

Kaleb looked at Noah and said, "God help us—we'll go—but if we haven't got something in a month, we'll come back here and try again—deal?"

Noah looked up excited, eyes shining in anticipation. "Yeah, yeah and if they don't want to pay us both—we'll tell them we'll work as a two'fer…2 for 1. How could they pass that up?"

Kaleb was less enthusiastic as they started off in the inky blackness. Whatever challenges they would encounter…he prayed that they would be successful.

It seemed like they had been walking for hours and he could tell Noah was slowing down a bit. Although he would never admit it to him, Kaleb knew Noah was struggling. He knew how much Noah looked up to him, how he was like the big brother he never had and although this made him feel proud, it also made him a little uneasy.

It was a big responsibility to be guiding and making pivotal decisions for him -what if he led them astray? What if he let him down? What if he put his life in danger? Kaleb turned to Noah and said, "Let's stop for a few moments, I need a bit of rest."

Gratefully, Noah sank down beside his friend. "Look there, Kaleb, the sunrise is so pretty."

"It sure is," Kaleb replied. Looking out into the distance, he silently prayed that God would look after them both on this journey into the unknown.

Chapter 2

The stiff wind howled through the cracked window and covered the woman sprawled on the floor. As the cold began to leech out her body heat, she began to stir, slowly pushing herself up. She looked cautiously around. The kitchen was in shambles, shards of broken plates and shattered glasses everywhere. Her right arm throbbed with pain and hung at an odd angle. Something warm and sticky was running in her eyes and she wiped at the blood absently as she continued to get her bearings.

Slowly, the memory of what had happened came back to her. Crying, she managed to stand up. A sharp pain in her ankle made her catch her breath. Looking down, it didn't appear to be broken…just severely strained. Leaning against the wall, she limped towards the other room. Following the sound of snoring, she came upon him.

Passed out, half in, half out of the chair, this man she called 'husband' was a pathetic sight. His shirt was torn and hung out of his pants. A trail of slobber and bile trickled down one side of his mouth. There was a large dark stain at his crotch—the odor making obvious what had happened. His knuckles were raw and bleeding from the beating he had given her and Noah…Noah—oh dear God…Noah—where was he?

Was he alright? Collapsing against the couch, she sobbed quietly, afraid to wake her husband. She prayed Noah had run away for good this time. She couldn't protect him anymore. She prayed he would start another life—a better one somewhere else. He still had a chance…unlike herself. She had chosen this life and must now make the best of it. Maybe if Noah was gone—maybe he wouldn't get mad all the time—maybe he wouldn't beat her so much— maybe he would be content to just drink and pass out—maybe…

Frantically gathering what little strength she had left, she limped from room to room searching for her son. Noah was nowhere to be found. Collapsing onto the bed, she prayed for God to protect her only child. He was in His hands now.

Chapter 3

They'd been walking it seemed forever; the sun was high in the sky and it was getting hotter and hotter. His shirt sticking to his slight frame, panting softly, Noah unbuttoned his shirt. "Hey—what's the rush, can't we just rest up for a bit?"

"You were the one all fired up about going," Kaleb said. "Don't be wimping out now."

"Come on Kaleb, ease up. Just a couple of minutes…I got to pee anyways."

"Well hurry up, we have to find somewhere safe for the night as we won't make the village before nightfall. We don't want to be out in the open after dark."

"Why…what's the problem?" Noah asked.

"There's wild dogs that prowl in packs and we don't have nothing to protect us with."

"You mean we could be in real danger, Kaleb?" Noah asked worriedly. The grim look on Kaleb's face said it all. Noah quickly zipped up and picked up the pace. Noah kept looking around for any dogs…but Kaleb was searching ahead for any possible hiding places.

The terrain had been getting rougher and more uneven so they had to start watching their footing more carefully. It would not be good to fall and twist an ankle. Not only would it slow them up…it could prove very dangerous in these unknown parts.

"You know Kaleb, we ain't got no money. I'm hungry and tired. We don't know anyone in the town…what are we going to do when we get there?"

"Will you just shut your trap?" Kaleb snapped. "We'll make do. We'll take odd jobs—work for food and lodging—ask for handouts…whatever we have to until we get on the boats."

Stumbling a bit, trying to keep up, Noah said, "Do you think we made the right decision to leave, Kaleb? Should we have stayed—maybe we should just go back?"

"Get one thing straight right now—you make a decision, you stick to it. That's what growing up means. Now stop whining and hurry up."

Pressing his lips firming together to stop any further outbursts. Noah stumbled on. Serious doubts clouded his young mind, but he would never speak of them again. Kaleb silently echoed Noah's fears, but he too, would never voice them. They had embarked on this journey with high hopes, but little preparation…they would continue until they could go no more. Although their future was uncertain—he knew that what they had left behind was even worse.

The sun was low and the air had a definite chill in it. They had walked all day and still no sight of the fishing village. They were tired and hungry. Kaleb was getting uneasy as he looked around at their surroundings. The rolling hills had morphed into hilly terrain with craggy outcroppings of rocks and stiff brush. He was aware of the dangers darkness brought out here and he anxiously searched for a safe place to spend the night. Not far ahead was a cluster of caves that might provide shelter from the weather—and whatever else might be out there. "Hurry up, Noah, we gotta make those caves before—"

A long howl pierced the stillness of the night and sent shivers up their spines. "What was that—holy shit—what was that?" Noah whispered.

"The dogs—I was afraid of that…run for those caves Noah…run as fast as you can!" As they ran through the deepening blackness, the air was filled with a chorus of frantic yelps and shrieks. There seemed to be many blood-thirsty hounds gaining on them. As they frantically raced towards the caves, Noah tripped and fell down hard, knocking the wind out of him.

"Get up, Noah, get up!" Kaleb yelled as he frantically pulled at him. Suddenly, the shrieks changed to low, guttural growls. It sounded very close— too close. "Run dammit, run. Don't look behind you, Noah, just keep running. We're almost there!"

Their fear was palpable as Noah began whimpering. On and on they ran, for what seemed like forever. Just when they thought they could go no further, they stumbled up to the first cave tripping over some rocks scattered about in front.

Diving into the darkness, they fell down a long tunnel. Screaming in fear and desperation, they twisted and tumbled trying to grasp at anything. There was nothing to hold onto…nothing to stop their descent. Their bodies scraped and bumped against the sharp walls as they finally came to rest at the bottom. Far above them, they heard the whimpering and frenetic scratching of the wild dogs. Relief that they had escaped the mongrels was short-lived as they realized their predicament. Scraped and bleeding, but thankfully with no broken bones, they reached out for each other in the dark.

"Are you alright, Kaleb, are you OK?"

"Yeah I think so—how about you?"

"Just shook up is all…what just happened?"

"We fell down some tunnel. I don't know where we are…let me think," Kaleb answered. Stretching out his arms, Kaleb felt the cold, wet ground. The rocks were slick with moisture and there wasn't much room to maneuver. Inching forward, he felt the space opening up a little. "I think we can go this way. Stay close, Noah…don't get lost."

Shivering, Noah let out a yelp as something slithered across his hand. "Don't worry Kaleb, I'll be right behind you." As they moved slowly forward in the total darkness each boys thoughts were filled with serious doubt. *It would do no good to panic now*, Kaleb thought…they must have their wits together if they were to survive. Inch by inch they moved along the narrow space.

Time lost meaning for the boys as they moved slowly along. "I don't like this, Kaleb…I can't see where we're going…what if we come to the end and can't go no further…what if the walls cave in, Kaleb? Oh my God, we'll die here!" Noah was getting hysterical.

"Noah, we are not going to die…take a deep breath and focus!" Kaleb said sharply.

Noah swallowed and tried to calm himself. Minutes later, Noah again started to cry. "Bats…what if there are bats, Kaleb? I can't take no bats, that will just finish me." He totally broke down and his body just gave out.

Kaleb looked back and could see his little body shaking. Feeling sorry for what he was going through, he said softly "Noah…there are no bats, buddy…we're in a tunnel…bats only live in caves."

"You really think so?" Noah sniffed.

Truth be told, Kaleb had no idea where bats lived, but they'd deal with them if they had to. His mum always said, "Don't go borrowing trouble

Kaleb…it will find you soon enough." Honestly, he was more concerned with whatever slithered in that darkness rather than flew in it, but he'd keep those fears to himself.

After a few minutes' rest, they continued to follow the tunnel unsure of where they were heading. They lost track of how long they had been crawling and the many twists in the tunnel had made them even more disoriented. They came to a fork and Noah said, "Which way Kaleb…which way?"

"Just a minute…let me think, dammit." One way seemed a bit slimier…so Kaleb decided to go that way in hopes of finding more water. He hoped finding the water source would give them the best chance to get out of there. Maybe it would turn into a river that they could follow out of this mountain. He realized it wasn't much of a plan, but they really didn't have any other options. "We go right."

After several minutes, Noah was gasping. "Wait Kaleb, I can't go no further."

Kaleb again questioned his decision to go on this fool-hardy journey. "OK, we'll rest for a bit." Truth be told, he was getting pretty winded himself. After a few minutes, they continued down the tunnel. He realized they seemed to be going upwards a little. This of course only made it harder for them. As they travelled further into the darkness, the grade rising steadily, the ground became wetter and slimier. It wasn't long until they were soaking wet.

They made a pitiful sight. Wet and shivering, muddy and covered with cuts and scrapes, they were miserable. They hadn't eaten since the day before and they're stomachs were protesting loudly. The lack of food and their continuing exertion made them nauseous and light-headed. Several times they were forced to stop and rest, as they were nearly spent…but the increasing sound of water gave them hope. Cold and exhausted they crawled forward…

Chapter 4

The sliver of sun barely shone through the cold morning dawn. Ester crept out of bed quietly to make a fire in the stove. Not wanting to wake the children, she stoked the embers and began the morning chores. Thankfully, she still had a hen that would provide eggs for breakfast at least. Milk was out of the question though—the baby would just have to settle for warm water with a bit of sugar.

Wearily, she sat down placing her head in her hands. What little food they had left would be gone in a few days—what would they do then? Things used to be better before her beloved husband passed. They still were dirt poor, but he always seemed to put food on the table. There were many happy evenings sitting around the little fire, singing hymns and rocking the baby.

He would be showing Kaleb how to sharpen blades and talking "man-to-man", while the older girls would be brushing each other's long silky hair. The twins would be curled up at her feet, content to watch it all. Yes, she thought, they had food and a warm house and most of all…love. Nothing else really mattered.

The twins appeared and clambered onto Ester's lap, snapping her out of her reverie.

Tears fell as she held them close to her. *God help us*, she prayed. Maybe Kaleb would find work soon.

She should wake him now and fix his breakfast first so that he would have the whole day to search for work.

Walking back to the little room, Ester saw the threadbare blanket on the mat pushed aside. Had he already left to find work? Surely he would have told her. Unable to spare any more time on this question however, Ester woke her remaining children.

The sun had finally broke through the clouds and the day was warming up. *Praise the Lord*, she thought, at least the girls wouldn't be cold as they walked to school this morning. Warm clothes and sturdy shoes were a luxury they didn't have, so every warm day was a blessing. Maybe today they would get their miracle, maybe today Kaleb would find work, maybe today their stomachs would be full, maybe…

Chapter 5

Slowly, they moved closer and closer to the sound of rushing water. They had been crawling for hours it seemed and the further they went…the louder the sound of water. Their hands were bleeding profusely from grasping at the sharp edges—their knees scraped and stinging from slipping and sliding their way through the tunnel, but they kept going.

Almost imperceptibly, the darkness surrounding them was getting less dense—the inky blackness was turning into shades of increasingly lighter grey. Hope resurfaced as they felt they finally might have a chance of getting out of there. Suddenly, up ahead they saw a pinprick of light.

"Oh my God! Look, there's light up there!" Noah excitedly said. They had been slowly creeping upward for some time now and the light surely meant escape from this dungeon. Tired, hungry and covered in mud, their freezing, aching bodies moved forward to the lip of the tunnel.

As they peered through the opening they saw the origin of the water. Cascading down a steep, slippery rock face was a bubbling, frothy wall of water.

They fell back exhausted and in shock. *Is this what they've been struggling for hours for?*

The only way out was up the jagged side of the cliff. The rushing water from the waterfall created steam that made the surface slick and dangerous. One slip, and they would fall to their deaths. The enormity of the situation overwhelmed them. Surely this was an impossible task. Both friends were silent as they contemplated what they were about to do.

Kaleb thought that Noah would never be able to do this—hell, he probably wouldn't either. Noah silently prayed that he would not disappoint his good friend. Looking down into the deep gorge, Kaleb cautioned Noah. "Don't look down, buddy. Take your time—make sure you have a good grip before you move."

Looking down into the swirling waters, Noah fell back against the tunnel wall—squeezing his eyes tightly. His thin, battered body was shaking in fear and exhaustion. "I can't to it, Kaleb, I just can't. I'll wait here while you go for help."

Kaleb was afraid of this. How could he talk Noah into doing something that he himself might not be able to do either? Sliding in beside him, Kaleb grabbed Noah's hand. Shouting to be heard over the raging waters, he turned Noah's head to look into his eyes. "I'm not leaving you Noah, there's no other way. We can't go back the way we came…this is it. We have to do this."

"I'm too weak, Kaleb—I'd never make it."

"Yes you can and you will!" Kaleb shouted. "Remember why we're here. Remember our family that's counting on us. They won't make it without our help."

Sobbing, Noah just kept shaking his head no. Kaleb was beside himself. How could he give courage when he had none to give? Feelings of regret and helplessness filled his head. He should never have agreed to this…Noah was just a boy…he should have refused, tried to talk him out of this reckless folly. If anything happened to him, it would fall on his shoulders. Exhausted, he laid back against the cold wall and shut his eyes, The tumbling waters had an hypnotic effect on the boys, and soon they fell into a fitful sleep.

He ran out of the house towards his Dad in the field. "Well now, son, are you going to help me plant today?"

"Yes Dad, can I?"

"As long as your Mum doesn't need help around the house, son, cause you know she's almost ready to give you a new brother or sister."

"A boy…it's going to be a boy, Dad." Smiling, his Dad ruffled Kaleb's hair. Farming was hard work that never seemed to end. His Dad was a good man who worked tirelessly for his family. He was still a young man in age, but the endless long days had taken its toll. He found it harder and harder getting up each morning.

He also had a variety of aches and pains that never seemed to leave him alone, but the last few days he was noticing something new. He had been having pains in his chest but kept that to himself. *No need to worry the missis*, he thought. Probably just a pulled muscle. He'd rub some ointment on it tonight and he'd be fit as a fiddle then. Right now though, they had to get these seeds in before dark.

Handing his first-born a hoe, he thought back to when Kaleb was born. They had only been married less than a year, but welcomed this little addition to their family. They named him Kaleb after his father and delightedly watched as he grew. He was a sturdy young child and very bright. Kaleb was the apple of his eye and he enjoyed countless hours just sitting and watching his antics…that was until the rest of his brood were born, pretty much back-to-back and then there wasn't much time left for anything!

As they worked side by side, the younger mimicking the older, time passed comfortably. Kaleb thought he had the best Dad in the whole wide world and loved spending as much time with him as he could. As he helped his Dad, Kaleb thought of his Mum and the baby soon to arrive. He sure hoped it would be a boy, as although he loved his 4 sisters—it wouldn't hurt to have another boy—just to even things up a bit, he laughingly thought.

Dad bent down to pull out a heavy branch from the field when suddenly his right arm felt numb. Standing up, be began to rub it, thinking he would just take a little break. "You OK, Dad?" Kaleb asked.

"I'm OK, Son…" Suddenly, a sharp pain ripped through his chest, and crying out, fell to the ground.

Kaleb screamed and dropped down beside him. "Dad, Dad, what's wrong?" Kaleb cried. As he looked up at the blue sky above, he thought he'd never felt pain like this before…unable to answer his son, he closed his eyes and surrendered to the pain.

Kaleb screamed for his Mum. Moving as fast as she could so close to her due date, she managed to get to them and slumped down sobbing on her husband. There was nothing that could be done. Kaleb's Dad had passed. The color drained from Kaleb's face as he sat there his head in his shaking hands.

Tears flowed freely from both Mother and son, as they realized they had lost this loving man. "We were just laughing together a minute ago," Kaleb sobbed to his Mum. Grabbing him to her bosom, the Mother rocked him back and forth as if he was a baby.

Kaleb was tasked with getting the doctor and that night became the longest of his young life. His Mom had to leave her beloved husband, lying there in the field as she had to take care of the other children. Before Kaleb left to get the doctor, she had him bring out a blanket to cover his Dad with. No crows were going to feast on this man she loved so much.

It was after dark by the time the doctor had arrived with the cart to transport his body. By the time Ester had explained to the children what had happened and calmed their tears, she fell into her bed alone for the first time. Her arm kept reaching out for him through the night, and each time she again relived the excruciating pain of that afternoon. As she wept, she prayed to God to get their family through the coming despair and hardships.

Two days later, she gave birth. What should have been a celebration, welcoming their new son into their family, was instead a solemn affair. In just under a week, they had buried Kaleb's Dad and welcomed his little brother. The family stood in front of a plain little headstone. The day was grey and cold, the newborn baby wriggling in Mum's arms. Things were never the same after that…

"Get your ass out here and make me breakfast woman…now."

Noah looked up at his Mum, her face puffy from the beating and also from the crying. He clenched his hands in frustration and crying, hugged his mother. "Shh honey, I'm OK…I'll fix his breakfast first so that he'll leave soon and then you and I will have some nice hot cocoa, OK?"

Noah shook his head but knew nothing would ever be OK…

Noah hugged himself and rocked back and forth. His heart broke for his poor mother. She was such a tiny little thing, soft spoken and gentle. She didn't deserve the life she was forced to live. How he wished the old bastard would just die. He was always in some bar fight, why couldn't someone just kill him? He knew these thoughts were not right, but God help him, he still prayed for it to happen.

Chapter 6

Sometime later, Kaleb woke up. No more feeling sorry for ourselves, he thought. We must continue—there was no other alternative. Grasping Noah's painfully thin frame, he shook him awake. As the sleep cleared from his eyes, Noah gasped. "I thought it was all a bad dream— Kaleb, what will we do?"

"We are going to climb out there and save ourselves—that's what we're going to do! Come on, Noah, you can do this. I will be right behind you." Truthfully, Kaleb felt sheer terror at what they were about to try, but knew he must be strong for Noah. "Remember your Ma—remember what that son-of-a-bitch does to her every day. You got to make money to get her out of there."

A look of determination came over Noah, as memories of the horror he'd seen came flooding back. "Yes, you're right, Kaleb, I will do this or die trying!" Noah's body was shaking, but he bravely positioned himself at the mouth of the opening. Freezing water immediately doused his body and he had to turn his head to catch his breath. He reached out and grabbed an outcropping with his hand. Almost immediately, his hand slipped off the greasy rock and he slid back down into the tunnel.

"It's OK, Noah, you're OK. I've got you. Just go slow, real slow. Make sure you have a good grip before you move. Remember, I will be right behind you." Admiration for him filled his heart as he knew how difficult this was for Noah. Silently willing for Noah to find the strength to try again, he waited. Again Noah reached forward. This time, his hand stayed secure as he lifted his body out of the tunnel.

Inch by inch, Noah slowly moved up the treacherous wall. Each time he found something to grab, he waited a few seconds to see if his grasp was secure. It was slow, tortuous going and his internal dialogue was unrelenting...(what the hell do you think you're doing, boy—you can't do this—you're just a spineless little sissy—you might as well just give in and do us all a favor...fall already!) "Shut-up...shut-up!" Noah screamed. The roaring thunder stole his screams away and Kaleb, only a few feet below him, heard nothing.

His fingers were turning blue and they began to lose all feeling. The freezing water was leeching out all movement and he was afraid he would not be able to grasp anything soon. Ignoring the old drunks commentary in his head, Noah was even more determined to do this, Instead of stopping him in his tracks and stealing whatever energy he had left…Noah staunchly kept going allowing it to spur him on.

Watching his ascent, Kaleb felt joy, love and admiration for his young friend (really like a little brother to him). What Noah lacked in size and experience, he more than made up with sheer determination and will. Kaleb was in awe of his bravery. It would spur him on to do the same. Tears of fear and frustration did not stop Noah from his climb.

As promised, Kaleb was right behind him. Suddenly Kaleb let out a frantic scream as one hand slipped off the rock face. He slid down several feet, until he again managed to get a secure hold. Gasping, he clung to his perilous perch, sucking in deep breaths. He too felt his whole body go numb and fear and desperation filled his mind. His body was almost spent.

Above him, Noah stopped and turned his head. "What happened, Kaleb, are you OK?"

"Keep going, Noah, I'm good!" Shutting his eyes tightly, he continued to catch his breath. I can do this, he told himself…I have to do this. Finally after what seemed like forever, Noah reached the top of the incline. Pulling himself over the ledge, his small body convulsed from exertion. Crying with relief, he lay inert on the ground. When Kaleb crested the lip, they hugged each other, both young boys thankful to be alive.

As they looked up at the early morning sky, they realized how lucky they were to have actually finished the climb. Suddenly, all the things that had never been important—now had tremendous value. The variations of blue in the sky…the smell of grass fresh from early dew, the feel of sweet-smelling air and the warmth of the sun drying out their sodden clothes.

"Oh my God," Kaleb sighed, "we made it—we actually made it. I thought we were finished there, I really did."

"What? I thought you said it was a cinch—not to worry," Noah said accusingly.

"Well, OK, maybe I exaggerated a bit. Who cares—we're here now, aren't we? We did it!" Taking long deep breaths, the boys lay prone gathering their strength.

Silently, each boy gave thanks to God for bringing them to this place safely. As they lay there gathering their strength, new sounds and smells registered. The sound of buzzing bees, the smell of salty air...the keening of gulls...wait...salty air...gulls...could they really be that close? Sitting up, they looked around in amazement. Off in the distance, in the valley below, was the little fishing village. They had crawled through the mountain instead of going around it.

Forgetting their hunger and exhaustion, they started running toward the village. What a sight they made—covered in filth, dripping wet, rushing and stumbling toward the village like lunatics! But a happier pair of lunatics you would never find!

Chapter 7

In the little fishing village, people were just beginning to stir. The gulls were swooping and careening over the dock looking for their breakfast from dropped pieces of fish from the last catch.

Essie had already made coffee when Jacob entered the kitchen. "Looks like it be a grand day for fishing, Pa."

"Aye, we should be lucky today, Ma." Although they were never blessed with children, they affectionately called themselves this, ever since they wed many years ago.

A fisherman's day was long and hard—but good work never hurt anyone—at least that's what Pa always said.

"We're almost ready for the season, Ma, just a few more supplies and we can set out." It was very unusual, unheard of really, for a woman to be part of a fishing crew—but ever since it was clear that the good Lord was not going to bless them with children, Ma said she wasn't about to waste away on land while her man was out to sea—so she accompanied him each season.

At first, the other mates were not happy to have her around. They felt it was no place for a woman—and some even thought she would bring them bad luck. After several years of plentiful catches and having proven she could carry her own weight, the guys not only accepted her—they grew to love her as well. It didn't hurt that she could whip up delicious meals from very little either!

"We should be ready to set sail by tomorrow's tide. I'll finish stocking the supplies this afternoon and then we'll have an early night." Pa left to get their tug ready while Ma started closing up their little house. They would be gone for a few months, so preparations had to be made. Little did they know that this trip would be like no other.

Chapter 8

He came awake abruptly with a thud as he fell to the floor. "What the hell? Where are you, woman—help me up, you old fool." She ran toward him as quickly as she could, considering the aches and pains she suffered from his beating. "Get me some coffee and make me some breakfast, I'm starving!" he shouted, as she helped him to the kitchen. As she worked quickly, he stared at her through rheumy eyes, bloodshot and watery. "Where the hell is that brat of yours anyway—tell him to get his ass over here right now."

"He's not here," she said quietly. "He's gone."

"Gone—gone where?" he demanded, rising half out of his chair.

"I think he's gone for good this time," she said, shrinking away from him. There was a moment of dead silence and she prayed softly, *dear God don't let him start again*.

Eyeing her dully through heavy-lidded eyes, the old drunk seemed to come to a decision. "Well good, I won't have to put up with that useless piece of crap anymore! And there'll be more food for me now too. But don't think you're getting off—you'll be doing his chores now too."

Silently, she gave thanks that Noah would no longer have to deal with his temper. A bit more work was precious little to pay for his safety. Obediently, she fixed breakfast and served the man she had come to hate. One day, she prayed, one day the Lord would deliver her from this hell on earth.

Chapter 9

As they came closer to the village, they slowed down and looked at each other. Immediately, they began to laugh. They couldn't go into town looking like this—not only would no-one hire them—they'd probably be run out of town! Their clothes were dark with filth and their hands were splattered with blood from the many cuts and scrapes they had gotten while crawling through the mountain. Their hair was matted and hung limply in their faces.

"What are we going to do, Kaleb, we look a mess!" Noah laughingly asked.

"Let's jump in the bay and wash off this grime. The sun will dry us off. We still might be a bit messy—but at least we'll be clean." Chuckling, they jumped into the water, clothes and all. Splashing around like fish, they played like children. Unknown to them, this would be the last time they would experience such innocent joy. Their world was about to be changed forever.

Climbing out, they wrung their clothes out as best they could and laid down on the bank. Their stomachs growled with hunger. but it was the best they'd felt in days. They dozed in the mid-day sun with the buzzing of bees in their heads, each dreaming their own thoughts.

Noah dreamt he would return home, big and muscular and kick the old drunk out for good. Kaleb saw himself returning with pockets full of money—filling his home with food and good cheer. Each boy dreamt innocent dreams. They didn't realize that life doesn't always have a happy ending.

Chapter 10

They'd just finished dinner and Ma was clearing the table. Pa had filled his pipe for his after- dinner ritual, when there was a hesitant knock on the door. As Ma opened the door, she looked at Pa with a 'who'd be coming by at this hour' look. Peering through the opening was what appeared to be a couple of orphaned children—raggedy and disheveled.

"Yes, can I help you boys?" Ma asked in a questioning tone.

"Well I, er, we would like to know if you would have any work for us?" the bigger lad asked. "It don't have to be big—anything would do. We're strong and we'll work for cheap."

As Pa came up behind her, they saw the younger boy shifting from side to side looking uncomfortable. "Yes, we'll do anything—we'll even work for food," he said as he hungrily licked his lips.

Shocked as she was, Ma stepped back and let them in. "Come in, come in, boys—you'll catch your death out there."

Ushering them into the warm kitchen, they looked at the boys closely. The older boy was tall and quite sturdy-looking. Hair tumbled out of his cap and he appeared to be the serious one of the two. The younger one was much more animated, eyes darting around the room, finally settling on the bubbling pot on the hearth.

Again, he licked his lips as he asked, "Ma'am, could we do some chores around here for a bit of that great smelling stew you have cooking?"

Ma could almost hear their rumbling stomachs as she said "Oh my, of course, you boys can share our meal. We have plenty left. Here, sit down and make yourselves comfortable while I get you some."

Pa sat down with them and watched as the lads dove into the stew, as if they hadn't eaten in days (which of course, they hadn't). "Where you boys from?" he asked.

"We're from Trenton, Sir, some 2 days over the mountain," Noah said between slurps of stew.

"Slow down boys—no-one's gonna take that food from you," Pa said with a bit of a chuckle. "You'll make yourselves sick."

Looking around the little cottage, taking in the warmth and delicious smells that surrounded them, Noah thought he was in Heaven. He had never been in such a warm and inviting place. The little cottage had a beautiful settee and two arm chairs placed in front of a roaring fire.

There were real cloth lamp shades with silk tassels and a pretty hooked rug underneath. As he looked into the faces of this older couple, he saw kindness and love. "Ma'am, this is the best stew I have ever had, truly it is." Noah sighed in contentment while he wiped his chin.

"Yes Ma'am, thank you kindly for sharing your food with us," Kaleb added. "We've been walking for days now, with little rest and no food. You're a lifesaver for sure."

"Oh my dears, it's a pleasure to share all that we have with 2 such nice lads. We don't get many visitors here, especially when we head out for the fishing season. You boys actually almost missed us, as we usually shove off today—but we had to get some more supplies. We'll be putting out to sea tomorrow now. Why have you young lads come all this way?" Ma asked.

"We've come looking for work, Ma'am."

"What kind of work are you boys looking for?" asked Pa.

"We want to be fishermen, Sir—we want to go to sea!" Noah said excitedly.

"Fishermen eh? Have you ever been on a boat?"

"Well no, but we're really strong and we learn really fast—and I know we'd love it!" Noah said confidently.

Trying to hide his amusement, Pa said, "It takes a certain kind of man to go to sea for long stretches. It's never the same twice. You have to go where the fish are—the weather can sneak up on you and your boat is thrown around like a toothpick, the waves can wash over the deck and take everything not tied down with it. It's a dangerous job. Long days of hard work and little pay if the fishing ain't good. It's not for the faint of heart."

"But that's the best part, Sir," Noah said excitedly. "We're up for the job, we wouldn't let you down, and we'll work as a two'fer—you'll only have to pay us one wage."

"Why would you be willing to work for half price, at such a demanding job?" Pa questioned.

"Sir, our circumstances are such that any amount of money would greatly help our families—and Noah is right, we'll work as hard as any other man you have," Kaleb assured him.

Pa seemed lost in thought for a moment. "Well now, we already have a full crew son, I don't know if we could fit in two more mates."

"Why don't we let these boys get some well-needed sleep, Pa, and we'll ponder it some?" suggested Ma.

"Alright, you boys can bunk in the back and we'll talk again in the morning."

After settling the boys up with warm blankets and good wishes, Ma returned to the living room. She heard the boys whispering to each other and she smiled. "Kaleb, have you ever slept on such a bed? And have you ever had fluffy pillows like this? I can't believe it…it's like we're in Heaven."

"Sure is wonderful…but you'd better get to sleep. We must be rested to face whatever is our fate tomorrow." Yawning, Noah agreed and promptly fell asleep. It was the best sleep of his young life.

Pa was stoking the fire as Ma came in and sat down on the couch. They sat together enjoying the warmth of the fire and each other's company. "What do you think, Pa, is there anything at all we could offer these boys? They seem so nice—friendly and determined to help their families. I'd sure hate to turn them away."

"Well, the young one can't be more than 14 or 15, could he even stand the rigors of ship life? Being nice is one thing, Ma, but it don't help none in a storm at sea."

"I know you're right, Pa," she sighed, "it's just—"

"Now don't be getting all swooned on me now—you ain't their kin, you know."

"I know, I know, but I can't help feeling something for that little Noah—he tugs at my heart. I just can't help it. And Kaleb looks like he'd measure up to any of our mates. He's strong and his heart is in it. He wouldn't have come all this way if he wasn't bound to do his best. Isn't there some chores they could do, Pa—things the other guys don't want to?"

A comfortable silence fell between them, as they both pondered what tomorrow would bring. Ma's thoughts went to the sadness in her heart, to have never been blessed with children of her own. Those boys appearing out of the blue, seemed like a gift from God. Just thinking of them sleeping in the back room, brought a smile to her face. Oh, how she hoped that Pa could find a place for them tomorrow on the boat.

Pa, on the other hand, wondered how they could justify bringing along two more mouths to feed, on an already crowded boat. He could see how important this seemed to Ma—and because he loved her so deeply, he would try to make this happen.

"I suppose they could fill in with cleaning and helping with the heavy stuff, at least until they learn the real jobs."

"Oh Pa, they'll be so excited—I can't wait to see their faces tomorrow when we tell them!"

"Our cut will have to be smaller this time—I'll not pay one to do the work of two."

"Don't worry dear, we'll make do—we always do," Ma said happily. "The joy of having those boys with us will make up for that."

Pa was not so sure. He knew the future was unpredictable and the days would be hazardous and exhausting. "I hope those boys haven't bit off more than they can chew," he said as they got ready for bed. The night was late and they had an early start in the morning. Falling into a restless sleep, he hoped he'd made the right decision.

Chapter 11

She stopped abruptly and leaned on the rake. Sweat shone on her deeply lined face as she took in deep breaths. She was not old in years, but the abuse she suffered for so long had taken its toll on her body. Although her friend had come over from the next farm to set her arm, her elbow ached dully as she tried to finish her chores.

It had been 3 days since Noah had left and her work had increased significantly. She now had to clean out the roost and take care of the pigs, on top of all her other duties. She shouldn't complain though, she thought, at least she had animals to care for—that would provide food for their table.

Poor Ester—all those kids and no way to feed them. She almost cried when she remembered the look on Ester's face when she had given her a chicken in thanks for her help with her arm.

Her face crumpled and she wept quietly as she accepted the offering. "Thank you, thank you—you have no idea what a Godsend this is. We'll have a wonderful meal tonight and this will feed my children tomorrow as well. This will be their first good meal in a long while. I pray our boys will return soon to help us out."

"Now Ester…promise me you will come back if you have no more food…I'll always make sure you have something to feed those children of yours. We are all in this together and the Good Lord would want us to share our bounty."

Gratefully, the two friends embraced. After Ester left, she continued her chores. It wouldn't be good if her husband returned and they weren't finished. Reluctantly, she began to once again rake, as her mind wandered back to when she had first met this cruel man she had married…

Chapter 12

The moon was full and there seemed to be a million stars shining brightly. It was a beautiful early fall evening. The fragrant aroma of clover and freshly cut bales of hay blended and wafted out into the evening air. The sound of crickets and the sparkle of fireflies completed the magical scene. The sound of music could be heard for miles over the silent valley and the sound of gaiety drifted out of the barn. Every year when the crops were sown, the town prepared a small feast and held a huge barn dance. This year, was the first time she was allowed to attend.

Sixteen and full of excitement, she entered the building. Sweet smelling bales of hay, covered with cloth were set up around the barn to sit on. There was a long, food-laden table with more food than she'd ever seen. Home-made apple cider (and brewed ale for the men) was also on hand. There was a band set up at the back of the barn and the middle of the floor had been swept for dancing. Giddy, she twirled around, her senses overcome with sights and sounds and aromas. She thought she would never be as happy as she was right this minute!

"Excuse me, may I have this dance?" a low voice said into her ear.

As she turned her head, she looked up into the bluest eyes she had ever seen. Blushing brightly, she nodded shyly. As she was swept onto the dance floor she wondered who this gentle stranger was. As they danced, he explained he had come for the harvest and travelled the country following the crops. The evening flew by, as she danced the night away in his arms. Round and round they twirled, each dance more heady than the last.

By the end of the evening, she was smitten. Taking a much needed break, they sat out under the stars and sipped their drinks. She couldn't stop glancing over at him. He was tall, broad shouldered and had curly black hair, with one lock that refused to stay in place. It continued to hang over one eye…which of course drew her to back to those shockingly blue eyes of his. As he swept her back onto the dance floor it was magical. Twirling faster and faster, she clung to him feeling breathless and giddy.

Is this what it's like to be in love? she asked herself. As he walked her home his arm around her lightly, she shivered with anticipation. Would he kiss her…would he want to see her again? She dreaded having to say goodnight. At her door, she looked up again into those eyes of blue. Wrapping her loosely in his arms, he gently lifted her up and gave her a soft kiss on her cheek. When he asked if he might see her the next night, her heart soared as she wordlessly nodded yes.

The days flew by and the evenings were long and tender. Their romance lasted until the first snow. When he sadly told her, he must leave to follow the next harvest her heart broke into a thousand pieces. Tears streamed down her face as she watched the love of her young life walk away.

Maybe if she had told him, he would have stayed. Yes, of course he would have—he was not the kind of man to leave a young girl alone at a time like this. But she foolishly did not want him to stay out of duty—she wanted him to stay for love. That was her biggest mistake. She allowed her vanity to make a decision that would forever change her life. She cried every night wishing she had told him.

What had she been thinking? What would she do now? Unable to put it off any longer, she finally told her mother that she was expecting a child. Her mother was distraught. "What have you done? What are we going to do? No-one will even speak to you if you have this child out of wedlock. Our whole family will be shunned—you will be despised. My God, what have you done?"

Several weeks went by. No-one spoke to her—she was invisible. Every night she cried herself to sleep. She prayed that God would help her. Day after day went by as she suffered in silence. Her mother would not even look at her. Her father had not been told, as he would have thrown her into the street immediately. They came from a long line of spiritual beliefs and life was strict and demanding.

They followed the Bible without question and sex outside of marriage was strictly prohibited. Their God was one of Fire and Brimstone—unforgiving and unrelenting. There were no exceptions—you were expected to follow their doctrines without question…or be thrown out of the congregation as well as your family.

One day her mother called her into the parlor. There, sitting stiffly on the settee, was an older man—cold and aloof. His eyes were hard and calculating. Waves of distain rolled off him as he looked her over. A chill ran through her as she returned his gaze. Her mother introduced him, saying that he was the answer to their prayers. The man was new to the area and was looking to settle and start a family.

Knowing of the young girl's situation, he had offered to marry her and claim the child as his. In return, she must never speak again of her lover and would care for him and bear his children.

She was horrified. Not only did she not love this man—he was old enough to be her father. And what of his demeanor? Not once had he even smiled or spoken kindly to her. He was dark and foreboding and he sent chills through her body as he stared at her with beady eyes.

"She will make a good vessel for my offspring, I feel," he said, as his eyes slowly travelled up and down her quivering body.

*This couldn't be happening. I won't do it...I won't...*she screamed in her head. *I'll run away...they can't make me...*

"We will be married immediately. I haven't got any time to waste. The crops must be planted and the house attended to." The young girl thought she would die. There was nothing she could do. Before she knew it, she was torn away from her home and living on a farm far away, isolated from everyone she knew.

The horror of her wedding night was relived every evening, as the man threw her down onto the bed. As he took off his suspenders, his eyes squinting in anticipation, he forced her to endure his demands over and over. "You'll do whatever I want, whenever I want, and you'll be thankful I took a little tramp like you in," he spat at her. There was no tenderness, no hugging or kissing— just animal lust. There were no words spoken—nothing to be said.

Days turned into weeks and the never-ending assaults on her body and self-esteem continued. Bit by bit she felt herself dying inside as she became a shell of herself. She found herself dreading each evening. She shuddered at the thought of what horrors he would bestow on her that night. How could this be happening? What had she done so wrong but fall in love? As she got bigger and bigger, her pregnancy more prominent, the old man began to lose interest in her.

Although she was grateful for this blessing, he took to staying out late and coming home drunk. One horror was replaced with another. Instead of forcing himself on her, he would now hit her and scream obscenities every night. Even right up to when she delivered her son, the verbal attacks continued. "You disgust me…look at you…your swollen belly shows what a little slut you are. Be very grateful that I rescued you from the shame you brought on…because no-one else would have even touched you!"

It was a miracle she had a healthy baby. He was the most beautiful boy with crystal blue eyes. Those eyes reminded her daily of the love she had lost. She would think of him every time she looked at little Noah and prayed that he would one day meet the loving man who was his father.

He never accepted the baby, never touched it—never even spoke to it. As the boy grew—so did his temper. And with each passing year when she failed to conceive his child, the old man grew meaner and more violent. Many nights she cowered in her room, trying to shield her son from his fury. He blamed her for not being able to produce a baby, not wanting to accept the obvious…that it was him, not her, unable to conceive. As the boy grew…so did the old man's fury. The sight of the beautiful little boy with the brilliant blue eyes drove the old man crazy.

As she shook her head to clear her thoughts, she saw how late it was and realized her husband would soon be home. Hurriedly, she finished the raking and stumbled into the house to prepare dinner. Dear God, she prayed, please protect Noah and keep him far from here.

Chapter 13

Hearing movement and whispers in the other room, Noah nudged Kaleb. "Wake up, Kaleb—I think they're in the kitchen." Kaleb yawned and stretched, wiping the sleep from his eyes.

Patting his full stomach, he felt content until he remembered what was at stake. "OK, OK, let's go find out what's going on." As they walked into the kitchen, Ma and Pa turned to them.

Coffee was brewing, eggs were frying and bacon was sizzling on the stove and Ma had just taken fresh rolls from the oven. The fragrant smells of breakfast made the boy's mouths water. Taking it all in, the warm and inviting scene brought tears to Noah's eyes—as this was what he'd always dreamt his life would be like.

"Oh dear, what's wrong, lad?" Ma asked as she put her arms around Noah's slight frame.

"Oh, it's nothing really…I just wish my home was like this."

"Dear boy, God gives everyone a different life to live—we can only do the best we can with what we have." Secretly, her heart broke at the longing in Noah's eyes. She prayed she would be able to fill the void that seemed to be in his life.

As the boys sat down at the table, Ma served them breakfast. Nervously, they looked at each other wondering what had been decided, but were afraid to ask. Pa, clearing his throat, began, "Now you lads must be anxious to know if we can help you or not."

Putting down his fork, Kaleb nodded nervously. Noah took a deep breath and the coffee caught in his throat as he sputtered and coughed. "Like I said, we don't need any more help. Our crew is complete and we're ready to shove off this morning."

Noah put down his cup and Kaleb started to get up. Their faces reflected their disappointment but they tried to hide their devastation. "Well, we thank you anyway for your kindness and we—"

"Now hold on there—I'm not finished," Pa said. As Kaleb sat back down, Pa continued, "As I was saying, we really don't need any more help—but Ma here has taken a shine to you boys and, well, I agree that you two seem to be really good lads. So we decided to make room for you and bring you along."

Whooping with delight Noah jumped up and hugged Ma. "Whoa there, take it easy, these old bones aren't that strong," Ma happily said.

"It's only starting out cleaning the deck and such—not a lot of money you know, but I will pay you both a day's worth. I won't take advantage of your good nature or desperate circumstances," Pa stated.

"This is more than we dared to hope for, Sir," Kaleb replied, shaking Pa's hand. "We won't let you down—when do we start?"

"Finish your breakfast. There won't be another like that for a while. You'll need some warm clothes. I'll advance you some of your pay. We'll go down to the store and get you boys outfitted. We'll leave right after that. If you lads want to write a note to your families—do it now cause we'll be gone a few months at sea."

Noah looked at Kaleb helplessly. He didn't know how to write and was too embarrassed to admit it. Kaleb, understanding, replied he would send a note for both of them. Kaleb hurriedly wrote his Mum and told her that Noah and he had found jobs on a fishing boat. He said they were setting off to sea and would be back by the end of summer. He told her he loved her and that he would come back with money to help them and for her to let Noah's mother know.

Following Pa to the trading store, the boys excitedly talked back and forth.

"I knew we'd get on a boat—I just knew we would," Noah whispered excitedly.

"Yea well, it's not going to be all fun and games you know. It's going to be really hard work," cautioned Kaleb.

"I know, I know—but Kaleb—we're going to be fishermen. I can't believe it—our dreams have come true!"

Kaleb silently hoped that they had not gotten in over their heads. They were just boys really—especially Noah. How would they compare to the seasoned crew who had done this for years? Would they be laughed off the boat, or even make a stupid mistake that caused someone to die? He couldn't be so blissfully happy as Noah—as the few years he had on him, gave him more insight as to what they were about to take on.

Chapter 14

Noah was like a little kid in a candy store. Eyes popping, he went up and down the shelves seeing all kinds of remarkable things. He couldn't hide his enthusiasm as he saw treasure after treasure. He'd never been in a store before—much less one that had everything he could think of. Everywhere he looked…around each corner there was some new and amazing find.

Pa looked on amused. Pa was reminded of how young and inexperienced these boys were. He hoped that his decision would turn out to be the right one. After buying what was needed, they met up with Ma at the boat.

As they got closer—Noah's bravado seemed to disappear as he saw a line of steely faces looking his way. Kaleb seemed to stiffen up and stand a bit taller in his shoes. He was afraid this would happen. What right did they have—2 young boys with no experience to just waltz in and expect to be accepted?

Pa sensed their hesitation and quietly said, "They all were young rookies at first too. Don't let them see you falter." One older man turned away and spat over the side of the boat. It was obvious he was not happy to see them. Another guy snickered to an older boy about 20 or so.

Well, Kaleb thought, *we have our work cut out for us just proving we belong here*. As they boarded the boat, he looked back at Noah. This would either make or break them, he thought. He hoped they were up to the challenge.

As the boat slowly left the dock, the gulls swooped down as if to say good luck. Pa called a meeting on deck with all the hands and proceeded to tell them about the boys. He was met with silence, as some of the men didn't seem to care about the kids' back story. They were unimpressed and uncaring. A few gave them a bit of a nod—but it was clear to everyone that they were not happy.

Seeing this, Pa said, "You guys are the best crew I've ever worked with. We are like family—we've been through so much together. Ma and I know your families and your circumstances, and you should remember that many of you came with similar stories. It is not where you're from—but where you're going to. Hard work and determination can overcome any hardship. All we ask, is that you give these boys a chance. They will determine whether or not they are cut out for fishing."

As the boat cut through the water, the boys just tried to stay out of the way as the crew began their duties. Pa had told them to relax today—just get their sea legs and they could begin tomorrow. The sky was a kaleidoscope of shades of blue and the enormous puffy clouds looked like you could almost reach up and touch them. The salty air seemed to invigorate them as they walked around the deck becoming familiar with the equipment. Wind streaming through his hair, the sun shining in his face, Noah couldn't stop smiling. What a rush—how lucky was he. His future looked bright.

Chapter 15

Looking up from the fragrant pot bubbling on the stove, Ester heard the girls rush in the front door. "Ma, we got a letter for you."

Ester put her spoon down and smiled. "You've got what?"

"A letter, Ma, Mrs. Eadie gave it to us at school. Quick, open it—open it."

Laughing, Ester turned the letter over. When she saw the address, her hands began to shake. Could this really be from Kaleb? Sitting down at the table, she carefully opened the letter.

Dear Ma, she read, *we've both got jobs on a fishing boat out of Tulin. We'll be back by the end of summer. Noah and I will save our money and make things better when we get back. Please tell his Mum not to worry. I'll take care of him. Love you lots—love Kaleb.*

As tears fell down her tired face, Ester was both relieved and worried for the boys. They were so young, how would they fair out to sea? They could sure use the money though. God Bless them and protect them she whispered as she took the stew off the stove. She must go right away and tell Noah's mother. She left the older girls to watch the younger children and set off for her friend's farm.

As she approached the small house, something felt wrong. Stopping, she looked around and realized there was no smoke coming from the chimney. That was odd, Ester thought, she should have been making dinner by now. Opening the front door, she saw the living room was in shambles. Furniture was toppled over and a broken lamp lay in pieces across the floor.

There was a smear of red across the wall, and coming closer she gasped. Blood—it was splattered everywhere. Cautiously, she followed its trail and as she turned the corner to the kitchen, she stopped. Fearing for her own safety, she hesitantly called out. No-one answered. Pots and pans were strewn across the floor and the metallic smell of blood filled her nostrils.

Moving farther into the kitchen, she saw a body sprawled on the floor. It was the old drunk. A dark stain was spreading out from under his head, as he lay unmoving. *Oh my God*, she thought, *he's dead*. Panic filled her as she frantically searched for her friend. Where was she? What had he done to her this time?

Suddenly, she became aware of whimpering. It was so soft, she almost didn't hear it. Looking around, her eyes focused in on a small heap curled up under the table. It was her friend. Stepping around the ever-increasing stain careful not to slip in it, she pushed aside the rubble to get to her. Ester's heart broke when she saw her old friend, softly mewing, rocking back and forth, staring out with blank eyes.

As Ester helped her up, she caught her breath. Her friend's face was almost unrecognizable. There wasn't much left of her nose and her face was covered in blood. Her lip was cut open and she was covered in bruises. Wrapping her arms around her gently, Ester was shocked at how frail her tiny shaking body was. Why, it was hardly bigger than her girls, she thought.

Feeling her bones as she held her, she actually felt as if she might break. She tried unsuccessfully to find out what had happened. Her friend could not speak. All she could do was cry and mumble incoherently. The smell of blood mixed with a strong odor of booze was sickening. Ester thought she might be sick. Trying not to gag, she continued to soothe her friend as she wondered what to do.

"It's OK dear—it's OK. Come along, hon—you're coming home with me. Everything will be alright." As Ester guided her through the house and down the road, the progress was very slow, as she had to stop every few minutes and let her friend rest. She thought to herself that it would never really be alright again. The walk home was long and difficult, trying to keep her friend upright along the uneven path in the darkening gloom. At times, she almost had to carry her.

Her friend had grown quiet on the journey back and seemed to be in another world. She appeared robot-like and Ester was afraid not only for her physical injuries—but for her emotional state as well. Finally, they arrived at her house. Taking her back to her bedroom, she shooed away the children clamoring around her full of questions.

"She's had a bad accident," she explained to her children. "Let me have some space so I can help her."

As the older girls kept the younger ones away, Ester tried her best to clean up her friend, but could do nothing for her broken nose. The girls would have to go in the morning for help. A doctor must be called and the police notified. Tonight, however, she would try to get her to eat a bit and then let her sleep. That's what her friend needed now most of all, sleep. Her friend would not eat, would not talk. It didn't seem as if she was even hearing Ester. Sadly, she simply left the room and hoped she would be a bit better after a night's rest.

Finally, after feeding, bathing and putting the children to bed, Ester sank down exhausted. As she reflected on what had happened that day, it seemed obvious. The old drunk had come home again and started beating her friend. It had probably started in the living room and continued into the kitchen. This time, however, it didn't end there. This time her friend must have fought back.

From the scene in the kitchen, she probably hit him with one of the heavy pans strewn across the floor. There was certainly no love loss for the old drunk. Silently, she thought it was a pity she hadn't done this years before. She continued to check on her friend throughout the night. There was no change. There was no response.

The next day the girls set off and returned with the doctor and the sheriff. As the doctor examined her friend, the sheriff questioned Ester. Stone-faced, he set out for the other farm. When he returned, he confirmed what Ester had thought. The old man was dead, obviously from a head wound. As it was common knowledge what had been going on for years, and because of her friend's multiple injuries, the sheriff believed it was self-defense.

There would be no need for a trial, however her friend would need to be hospitalized for observation and further on-going treatment. Ester had managed to get her to take a few sips of soup, but there was still no response from her. Her eyes were lifeless and she uttered no sounds.

Shaking his head sadly, the sheriff said she would have to be placed in an institution until she recovered—if she ever did. She had been through so much in her life and this might have been the last straw. She may never come back from wherever she had escaped to in her mind. The nearest facility that could handle cases like this was many miles away and Ester, fearing she may never see her again, hugged and kissed her cheek.

Before they led her away, Ester read the letter from Kaleb and told her Noah was fine and would come to see her when he returned. She had hoped the mention of Noah would illicit a reaction from her friend. There was no response. She could only pray that somewhere, deep inside, her friend had heard and was comforted. Sadly, she watched as her dear friend was led away.

Chapter 16

The morning was overcast and the boat was rolling in the churning waves. What started out so brightly yesterday—now seemed to be dark and scary. Noah had been awake for some time now, trying to quell the uneasiness of his stomach. Each time the tiny boat lurched, so did his stomach.

"Kaleb, are you awake?" he whispered.

"Yea, what's the matter?" Kaleb answered sleepily.

"I don't feel so good—I feel like I'm going to puke."

"Well, don't do it in here, we'd never hear the end of it. Go up and do it over the side of the boat."

"But I'm wobbly, I don't think I could make it. Besides, it's cold and dark out there."

"Alright shut up, I'll go with you." Slipping out of his bunk, Kaleb grabbed Noah just as he was sinking to the floor. Noah let out a low moan. "Be quiet, you idiot, we don't want the others to see this—they'll laugh us off the boat. Come on, get up."

They made their way in the semi-darkness up to the deck. The wind was sharp as it cut through their clothes like a knife. The deck was pitching at a wide angle and they had to hang onto the ropes to stop from being thrown overboard. No-one was seen as they shuffled carefully over to the side of the heaving boat. Noah leaned over just in time, as Kaleb kept a secure hold on him. Noah emptied his stomach. Wiping his face with shaking hands, Noah looked pale and very ill. Kaleb softened as he helped him back to his bunk. "Don't worry, kid, you'll feel better soon. You just need some rest."

"But why aren't you sick, Kaleb—you've never been on a boat before either. It's not fair that I feel like I'm dying."

"Oh you're not going to die, Noah. It might take a day or two, but then you'll feel fine. And me? Well, I guess I was just born with sea legs. Anyway, just lie down and try to sleep. I'm sure Ma will know what to do when she gets up."

As Kaleb entered the little eating area later, he saw everyone was already there. Ma looked up and saw the spittle left on him from Noah's early morning adventure. The others also saw what had happened and tried, unsuccessfully, to hide their amusement. The younger lad, however, laughed out loud.

Ma scolded him, "Now hold on Edward, it wasn't so long ago that you done the same thing, or have you forgotten already?" As the others laughed at this, Edward looked sheepish. He cleared his throat and went back to this breakfast.

"Kaleb dear, come in and sit down. Tell Noah not to feel bad, the sea affects everyone differently. There's no shame in getting your sea legs slowly at first. Bring him a dry piece of toast and a warm cup of tea when you're finished your breakfast. He'll be feeling ship-shape in no time. When that nasty storm has blown over and Noah is feeling a bit stronger, bring him up on deck to get some fresh air. Pa is at the helm right now, and says we have a few more hours of the squall, and then we should be good. Tell Noah to stay in bed until the weather breaks and then walk around the boat a few times—he'll be fine. And Kaleb?"

"Yes Ma?"

"Finish your breakfast, because once the storm ends—there'll be plenty to do."

After he had cleared his plate, Kaleb brought the toast and tea back to Noah. Helping him sit up, he watched as Noah nibbled his toast. Kaleb assured him that no-one was upset with him and that Ma had said for him to lie back and rest. She would check on him shortly and that once the squall had passed, he would bring him up to get some fresh air.

When he returned to the kitchen, most of the crew had cleared out and went back to their bunks. There wasn't much they could do until the sea had calmed down. Only Ma and Edward had remained.

"Look, I'm sorry I made fun of your friend there—Ma was right, I was just as bad," Edward admitted.

"It's alright, I appreciate the apology, there is lots for us to learn. But what we lack in experience—we make up for in determination. We won't let you down. You'll get an honest day's work from us and then some."

"OK, enough said. When the weather breaks, come up and I'll show you how to trim the sails."

"Thanks Edward, really appreciate that." The guys shook hands and returned to their bunks.

Chapter 17

By mid-day, the sky had cleared some and the swells had settled down. Kaleb followed Edward up and began his education on running a fishing boat. Venturing out of the bowels of the boat, Noah stepped carefully unto the deck. "Well young lad, you finally made it up here," Pa said in an understanding tone. "Just walk around the deck a few times and make sure you have your sea legs. When you're comfortable, you can swab down the deck. There are some nets that need fixing too."

Walking around the deck, there was so much to learn. Noah's head was swimming and he felt overwhelmed. How would he ever remember all this?

As Noah did a few laps around the boat, he felt a little better each time. This wasn't so bad, he told himself. Maybe this would work out fine. The boys settled into the rhythm of the boat and by early evening, most chores had been done.

"Edward, show the boys how to secure the supplies, and then get yourselves down for supper," Pa said, as he tied down the wheel. "We should have a quiet night hopefully."

Kaleb put his arm around Noah and told him he'd done great! Noah smiled and thought he just might get this yet!

After supper, someone pulled out a weathered harmonica and began to sing some old drinking songs.

One of the crew pulled out spoons, and the fun continued with everyone (except Noah and Kaleb as they had never heard of any of them) joining in. Edward explained there was no alcohol on board, except for medicinal purposes but that didn't stop everyone from having fun. By the end of the night, both boys could sing along, and Noah showed he had a beautiful singing voice. He laughed at that, as he had never even tried to sing a note in his entire life.

Mind you, his abusive childhood was not conducive to anything remotely to do with gaiety in any form. This random thought brought him right back to the night he'd left. *Oh Ma, I pray he has lightened up on you a bit. Hopefully now that I'm gone…there won't be that 'trigger' constantly in his face.*

Noah knew the whole story of his parents' love affair…that his birth father was a gentle soul with the most amazing blue eyes that his Ma had ever seen…and when she looked into Noah's eyes, he could see it brought her moments of loving memories. God knows, she needed those moments, however few.

Snapping out of his thoughts, Noah again joined in the fun. As Pa went up to have his nightly pipe, Ma finished up with the dishes and joined him up on deck. "Oh Pa, ain't never seen a more beautiful sky. Looks like you could reach out and grab a few of those twinkling lights," Ma said as she leaned into her husband.

"Aye, it's grand alright. Too bad she don't stay like this all the time. How do you think those boys did today—were we right in bringing them along?"

"I think they did real good, Pa. Noah, poor lad was suffering pretty bad there for a while, but once he got through that—he took to the boat real well. And Kaleb had his sea legs from the very start. He's a real natural. They both put in a good days work I reckon."

"Aye, you're right and the crew seems to be accepting them more too, so all-in-all I'd say things are working out pretty good. Tomorrow though, will be a true test, as we'll arrive at the fishing lanes. Then the real heavy work begins. We'll see how they handle that."

Chapter 18

Ester sighed deeply as she wiped the last bit of crumbs from the table. It had been over a week since they'd taken her dear friend away—and no further news from the boys. She hadn't sent word to Kaleb yet about what had happened, as she hoped she could send some positive news about Noah's Mom—but hadn't heard anything from the institution yet.

As she sat down, she marveled at what the last week had meant to her. She had been blessed on one hand, but broken-hearted on the other. When they placed her friend in hospital, the sheriff had visited her. Although she was still uncommunicative, it was determined there was no other family around.

As there was no-one else to care for her animals, the sheriff decided that the animals left unattended, would be given to Ester. Within one week, Ester's fortunes had changed dramatically. Instead of literally coming close to starvation, she now had a cow, 4 pigs, and several chickens. She now had a steady source of milk for her baby, and could even make cheese to sell in town.

With the extra chickens, she could also sell fresh eggs and make a bit of money. She could now afford to buy some warm clothes for the children and sturdy walking shoes. She was astonished at how her life had changed. Her prayers had been answered—but at what price? Her only friend in the world was far away—perhaps never to return. She had lived her whole life at the hands of an abuser, forced to suffer in silence, and now she was suffering again in a self-imposed silence. It didn't seem fair.

She was released from one prison—only to be put in another. Although she was so grateful for the blessings she had received, Ester couldn't help but feel guilty as well, as it had come from her friend's misfortune.

And what would she say to Noah? That poor boy had never really had a real father—someone to love and look up to. And now the only family he had left was locked away, likely never to return. How much could one small boy take? As Ester prepared her children for bed, she sent another prayer of thanks, and asked to be given guidance.

It was very early morning and the sound of loud barking woke Ester up. *We don't have a dog*, she thought groggily as she stumbled out of bed. Straining to identify the sound, she realized it wasn't barking, but coughing and it was coming from the baby's crib. *Oh my God*, she thought, as she grabbed her little baby. *Please God, don't let it be the croup.*

His little chest was heaving and his skin was burning up. As she rocked him gently in her arms, his deep coughing woke up one of the twins. Shooing her back to bed, Ester brought the baby into the kitchen.

Placing the sick infant down, she quickly started a fire and put a pot on to boil. Gathering up lard and spices, she made a poultice to rub on his tiny chest. Crooning to him, she held him close to the pot hoping the rising steam would clear his cough. Continuing to rock him gently, she rubbed and patted his back hoping to break up his congestion.

Morning came, to find her still in the kitchen, rocking the baby. He had finally fallen into a fitful sleep—but his skin was still hot to touch. Tears of frustration and exhaustion fell, as Ester repeatedly wiped him down with a cool cloth. It was a losing battle. As soon as she wiped him down, he was hot again. It seemed hopeless. She knew he needed medicine.

She woke her oldest girls and said they must hurry to town and bring the doctor back. He would make her son better—she was sure of it. She carefully put her son down and made a quick breakfast for the girls. As they set out for town, Ester prayed that everything would be alright.

As she made breakfast for the twins, she kept a close eye on her son. He was still sleeping, but his little body shuddered with each shallow breath. When she again picked him up, she panicked, as he seemed hotter than ever.

Trying to remain calm, Ester removed all his clothes and placed him in the sink. Splashing cool water over his burning skin made him cry out in pain. It must feel like torture, she thought, but she had to bring his temperature down.

Over and over, she repeated the ritual—splashing him and patting his little body to try and break up his congestion. Nothing seemed to help. Time seemed to stand still. She was beginning to give up hope, when she heard footsteps outside.

Chapter 19

Lying in the dark, swaying with the gentle waves, Ma's thoughts turned to years ago just after she had married Pa. They were so in love and he was a good man. One day he would inherit his father's boat and their future seemed secure. She thanked God daily for bringing this wonderful man into her life. Each day was better than the last. They would stay up late into the evening, watching the fire burn out in the hearth, each revealing more and more about each other.

Pa said he hoped to be as good a Captain as his father. The whole town thought highly of his Dad and he had taught his son to be a fair and righteous man. Ma shared her dreams of having children to love and an heir for Pa to leave the family business to. Every morning, bright and early, Ma would fix breakfast and send her love off for a day on the boat. Soon it would be fishing season and Pa would be gone for long stretches at a time. Wouldn't it be grand if she had a wee baby to care for while he was gone?

Until that time, Ma put all her efforts into making their little cottage a home. She found furniture that had been thrown out and lovingly restored them. She made beautiful lamps using bits of left over materials and she hooked a lovely warm rug to place in front of the fire. She decorated their bedroom in whites and rose gold and the second bedroom would be, she hoped for a wee one. She sewed and knitted and cooked and cleaned and was ready to start a little family.

Each day brought her joy and she continued to thank God for her blessings. The evenings were blissful as she grew more and more in love with this wonderful man. The only thing missing in her charmed life, was the pitter-patter of tiny feet.

Essie was beside herself—she was with child. She had never been happier. Tonight, she would make her husband's favorite meal and stoke up a blazing fire. She would share with him the wonderful news and they would celebrate.

Everything would be perfect. The table was set, the pot bubbling on the stove and a roaring fire in the hearth. Jacob would be home any minute now…

Suddenly, Essie doubled over as a searing pain pierced her stomach. Clutching her middle, she tried to catch her breath. Before she was able to straighten up, another wave of pain washed over her. Falling down, she began to moan in pain. The pain was so intense she did not notice the warm wetness spreading out beneath her. Never had she felt such pain. Her brain was racing…her heart beating wildly…*please God, please let our baby live…*The agony was so intense, she did not hear the door….

Humming softly to himself, Jacob opened the door. His nostrils flared as the aroma of his favorite food wafted out from the kitchen. Life was good. He had married the love of his life, had a job he loved and they had just bought this little house. It wasn't very big, but Essie said it was perfect. Besides, when they started a family, they could always get something bigger. His heart melted when he thought of how much Essie had done with their little house. What a great mother she would be if they were blessed with children. That would be their crowning glory.

As he turned the corner and entered the kitchen, his smile turned to terror. There on the floor, Essie lay in a small heap unmoving. "Essie, oh my God, Essie what's wrong?" She did not answer. Rushing over to her, Jacob noticed the puddle beneath her. " My God, what is this?" he cried, as he picked her up.

The sudden movement revived Essie and she began to moan. Panic engulfed him as he carried her to their bedroom. As he gently laid her on the bed, covering her up with a blanket, he said he was going to get the doctor. He kissed her and said he loved her and would be right back. She didn't answer— she didn't move.

He ran out the door and down the hill to the village. Although it was only a few minutes from their home, it felt like hours before he reached the doctor's door. Pounding wildly, he waited impatiently for the door to open. Explaining what happened, the doctor grabbed his satchel and followed Jacob. When the doctor asked if she could be pregnant, Jacob said, "No, I don't think so—she would have told me."

Arriving at the house, Jacob brought the doctor into the bedroom. After shooing him out of the room, Jacob paced back and forth. Could it be true? As he waited impatiently, he recalled all their past conversations about starting a family. They dreamed of the time when the patter of little feet would run through their home. They agreed that nothing would be better than to be blessed with children—how it would complete their lives. Suddenly very afraid. he started to shake.

As the doctor came out, he guided Jacob to a chair. "Sit down son, we'll have a little chat." Jacob's hands were sweaty and he rubbed them absent-mindedly on his pants. As he looked into the doctor's sad eyes, he knew the news could not be good. "Your wife was indeed pregnant, Jacob, but I'm very sorry to tell you she has lost the baby. The baby was very small, only a few weeks old and these things happen sometimes. There was nothing she did wrong—nothing anyone could have done to prevent this. She's lost a lot of blood and is very weak. She must stay in bed for at least a week, and you mustn't let her do anything."

"She's going to be alright though, doctor?"

"Yes, she'll be fine. I was able to stop the bleeding and she's out of danger. However, I have more bad news. I'm afraid she will not be able to conceive again. The damage was irreversible. I'm so sorry, Jacob."

Jacob's mind raced as he saw the doctor to the door. What would he say to Essie? How would he comfort her? They'd had such hope for the future—so many plans. Children, lots of them, had always been part of them. As he slowly walked towards the bedroom, gathering his thoughts, he prayed he would find the words to help his wife. Entering their room, he saw that Essie was curled up into a tiny ball and looked asleep.

Looking around, he saw the mound of bloody sheets and he realized the enormity of what had just happened. His big heart shattered into a million pieces as he gazed with love at his young wife. Trying to hold back tears, he softly asked, "Are you awake, dear?" A small cry escaped her lips, as Essie turned to her husband.

"Jacob, I'm so sorry. I was going to tell you tonight. It was supposed to be a big celebration, but now…" her voice caught and she began to cry.

"There, there, darling, it's alright. You're going to be fine—we both will be fine. We'll get through this together. Everything will be OK." He wrapped his arms around her as she sobbed.

"But Jacob, we can never have children—what will we do? How will we survive never to hear little ones at our feet? I can't imagine my life without wee ones. God help me, Jacob, what good am I if I can't have your children? Do you even still want to be married to me?

Jacob took her beautiful face into his hands. "My God, Essie, it's you I love. That will never change—always and forever. If we are meant to be childless, then we will find other ways to share our love. I don't know what the future holds, but we will follow the path the Lord has chosen for us." Rocking back and forth, they fell asleep with whispers of undying love on their lips.

Chapter 20

The first few weeks were the toughest and Jacob tried to show his love and support every day. Essie found herself feeling sad and depressed. Although Jacob reassured her over and over that it would be OK—it didn't feel like it ever would. On one of her first excursions into the little village, she came upon a young mother pushing a baby carriage.

Bursting into tears, she raced back to her house and collapsed on the bed. Deep sobs racked her body as the reality of what she could never have hit her. I can't do this, she silently cried to God—I can't handle the pain—the loss. God help me, I don't want to be here anymore. As she continued to sob into her pillow, a picture of Jacob came into her mind.

Jacob getting down on one knee to propose to her, Jacob carrying her over the threshold on their wedding night, Jacob crying with her and telling her how much he loved her. She sat up and looked around the room. She suddenly felt a calmness come over her. Drying her eyes, she gazed upon the family Bible beside the bed. It had been her mother's…and her mother's mother.

She picked it up and began to read… Ever since she felt the urge to read her Bible, Essie had begun to get stronger and more determined to get on with her life. She gave thanks each morning for a loving husband, a warm and cozy cottage and the blessings of good health that was bestowed on her. But even with her new-found mindset, Essie found it very hard to be alone during Jacob's fishing excursions. The days were long and the nights longer still.

Unwanted thoughts would spring into her mind, and she was afraid she would slip back into a deep depression, even with the solace she got from reading her Bible every day. She began to talk to Jacob about joining him on the boat. At first, he was hesitant and thought it would not be a good idea.

He wasn't sure if Essie was physically strong enough, or if the crew would even take to her. The more Essie pleaded with him, the weaker his resolve became. Finally, he agreed to a short trial-excursion. If she proved she could handle it, and if the crew agreed—she would accompany them during their next fishing season.

That was many seasons ago, and eyes fluttering, Ma was back in the boat again. Why was she thinking about all of this now? What had stirred those long forgotten memories? Even before the question was fully formed, she knew the answer. Noah—that young lad who had shown up on her doorstep, as though Heaven-sent.

What was it about him that stirred her so? Why did he have this effect on her? Several boys had come into her life throughout the years, but none had the impact of Noah. Feelings of emptiness, loss and ever present sadness were mixed with hope and the possibility of fulfilment. Deep maternal instinct rose from within. Was this the Lord's answer to her repeated prayers?

As morning broke. she decided to stop trying to explain her feelings and just accept this chance to experience what she felt was the greatest calling on earth—parenting. She felt somehow, that this boy was in desperate need of nurturing. She would embrace what she felt was God's second chance to mother a child. A contented smile on her weather-beaten face, she fell back into a restful sleep.

Chapter 21

Noah awoke with a start. Listening, he heard the waves slapping against the boats hull. Craning to see in the darkness, he could barely make out Kaleb's body in the next bunk. His life had taken so many turns lately, he didn't know what to make of it all. Thinking back to the night he left—it all seemed so long ago. He remembered the old man shouting obscenities and coming towards him. He could feel the wind being knocked out of him as he fell to the floor.

Bending over him, the drunk spat in his face. Still dazed, he saw his mother grab a broom and move towards him. As the drunk's foot connected with his stomach, he heard the sound of wood cracking. "You'll not touch my boy once more—God help me—you won't."

Howling, he turned and grabbed her hair. Noah's mother screamed as he smashed his knuckles into her face. Falling back against the wall, she slid down to the floor. Picking her up, he threw her into the table. Chairs toppled and dishes flew. As Noah struggled to get up she pleaded, "Noah, run, get out. Please dear God, just go!"

Weaving unsteadily on his feet, the old man swerved around and screamed, spittle flying from his mouth, "I'll kill you, you useless brat. I should have done it long ago. I'll kill you and your whore of a mother." Noah, enraged, ran towards him.

Slamming into him, the drunk fell into the wood stove. He howled as a pot of boiling water splashed over him. Grabbing his right side, he stumbled into the living room and passed out.

Rushing over to his mother's motionless body, he feared the worst. Her hair was matted with blood and her arm hung at a weird angle. As he picked up her limp hand, she began to moan. "Run son, run," she murmured.

"I won't leave you, Ma, I won't."

"Please Noah, it'll be easier on me if you go, please," she begged. Looking around at the destruction, his mind was racing.

How many times had this happened? *How many more times will it take before the bastard actually kills her? But maybe Ma was right. Maybe if I wasn't here, I wouldn't be a constant reminder of his mother's true love.* Maybe the old drunk would take it easier on her if he wasn't there.

A minute went by and Noah seemed to come to a decision. Leaning close to his mother, he whispered into her ear, "I don't want to leave you, Ma, but maybe you're right. I can't watch him beat you anymore. I'll go, but when I come back, I'll make sure that bastard never touches you again. I love you, Ma. I'll pray for you every night." Kissing her gently on her battered face, he turned away quickly before she could see the tears start to fall. With a catch in his throat, he walked out the door. As he left the little farmhouse, he wondered what lay in store for him.

Desperate but with no plan and no destination, he walked off into the deepening night.

Blinking quickly, his eyes bright with unshed tears, Noah was once again in his bunk. Getting up, he prayed his mother was alright. Kaleb began to stir and rolled over. "What time is it?" he asked groggily.

"Don't know, but I'm heading down to the galley."

"Hold on then, I'll come with you." Rubbing the sleep from his eyes, Kaleb followed Noah down the hallway. Greeting the others at the table, the boys sat down.

"Well mates, this will be our first full day fishing. Eat up and dress warmly—there's lots to be done. Noah, you'll be busy keeping the decks clean as they pull in the nets. Make sure you swab them good—don't want anyone to fall into the sea," Pa chuckled.

"Edward, you show Kaleb how to work the nets, he'll be your helper today. We'll work as quickly as possible, as the weather can turn on us pretty fast." They hurriedly finished their breakfast and began to leave.

Ma turned to Noah as he was rising from the table. "Don't worry, lad— you'll do fine. Just stay out of the way of those sails. They can sweep a man out to sea if you don't see them coming."

"Don't worry, Ma, I'll be careful—and I'll do a good job, just wait and see," he said excitedly.

"Aye, I know you will," she said as she gave him a quick hug.

As he clambered up the stairs, anxious to become a man, she thought—he was so young—just a boy really. God help him and keep him safe.

The deck was filled with activity. Everyone was busy doing their job. Noah was so thrilled, he didn't know where to look first. "Look out—pass me them gloves."

"I need some help over here."

"Watch it—grab that line."

"Kaleb, pull the rope up—that's it, keep pulling," Edward shouted. Kaleb leaned over the side of the boat and pulled with all his might. He thought his back was about to break. Finally, the net began to move. Slowly, it inched upward and it was all hands on deck to bring it into the boat. The net was teaming with jumping fish.

Noah laughed excitedly, having never seen anything like it. As they emptied it into the hold, other guys started to shovel salt over the catch. Throwing the net back into the sea, they moved on to the next one. They repeated this over and over until mid-day, when they stopped for lunch and a much needed rest. Edward slapped Kaleb on the back. "Good job, Kaleb—you did great."

Kaleb, although aching from head to foot, felt such a sense of accomplishment. Noah came rushing up, wet and covered in fish slime—but with a grin from ear to ear. "Wow, this is great—we're fishermen!"

Laughing, Kaleb got up to go back to work. "Yep, it's pretty fantastic." As Edward and Kaleb walked over to the side of the boat, someone thrust a mop and bucket into Noah's hands. "Start rinsing the deck down, boy, or we'll all fall off the boat."

"Aye, aye Sir," Noah said. "Right away, Sir!" Noah quickly began to clean the blood and slime away, humming to himself. He had never felt so happy or alive. The crisp air, the salty spray off the sea, the sun beating down—it was all so invigorating.

The gulls screeched as they swooped down over the little tug, hoping for leftovers. Everyone was working hard, but loving it at the same time. Even Ma joined in, manning the wheel while Pa was netting with the others.

Chapter 22

As the day got longer, the sun was unrelenting as it got hotter and hotter. Clothes were ripped off, layer by layer as the crew struggled in the heat. It was unusual for it to be this hot early in the season—and it was taking its toll on the men. Sweating and panting, they could almost smell their skin crisping up under the scorching sun.

Pa ordered them all to cover up and to make sure they were wearing their hats, as he didn't want anyone getting heat stroke. Noah's baby skin took a beating, his back was bright red from the sun and large water blisters broke out adding to his pain. Every time he flexed the muscles on his back to swab the deck, it seemed another blister burst, leaving open sores. When the salt water splashed up, he was in agony.

Suddenly, Noah wasn't so glad to be a fisherman. Trying to hold back tears, he kept going. Each time a blister broke, however, he had to stop for a minute and catch his breath.

The pain was never-ending. Seeing this, Ma spoke to her husband. He agreed he should stop for the day and go down and get out of the blistering heat.

When Ma told Noah he was to go down to his bunk, lay on his stomach, and she would make a soothing poultice to ease his pain, his relief was obvious. As he went down into the sleeping quarters, Ma told him to relax, she would be back soon. Lying there in the semi-darkness, Noah could not remember a time that he had ever felt pain like this—not even after one of the old man's beating. He had felt pain too many times in his young life, but never like this.

In the little galley Ma hurriedly threw together some lard, spices and cooling mint leaves (thankfully, she'd brought some this time from her little garden at home), and ground them all together. She should have watched him more closely, she chided herself, she should have made him put his shirt back on. He couldn't have known the dangers of uncovered skin in these situations, but she did. *Now look what he must go through. It could be days until his back is healed enough for him to rejoin the others.*

Coming up to Noah, she told him this would feel lovely and cool. As she carefully placed the poultice on his burning back, he sighed with relief. He must remain on his stomach, at least until tomorrow, and possibly a day or so after as well, depending how well the poultice worked. She would return every couple of hours to replace the poultice and check on him. Until then, she told him to try and rest up.

She kissed him on his cheek and went back up to help the others. Noah drifted in and out of consciousness. His dreams were pain-addled and they jumped from one memory to another. The old man dragging him outside in the early morning to chop wood…making him stand outside in the pouring rain because he…(couldn't even remember why)…the night the old drunk had passed out on the front porch and his Mum had made him help him into the house (should have just left him there, he thought)…the time the old bastard had showed up at school, ranting and raving that it was all a waste of time and then dragging Noah out as everyone else backed up and watched in horror…his Mum rocking him to sleep when he was a little boy…how she used to read him stories softly, so as not to wake up the old drunk…all of these flew across his mind in his fitful sleep.

As Ma stepped on deck, she heard Pa warning the crew. He said this sudden fierce heat wave might bring with it a severe storm. He looked warily at the changing sky. The sky was a peculiar steel grey and there were suddenly no birds keening overhead. Pa knew the absence of the birds was not a good thing. "Hurry up and finish the nets, I think this will be a bad one."

The crew worked together for another couple of hours, until the last net had been emptied. There was no bantering back and forth between them, as they too had a bad feeling of what was to come. As they began to batten down everything as Pa had told them to, they saw the sun had disappeared and was replaced with large, ponderous clouds that looked ready to burst. As they finished, they felt the first droplets of water and noticed the waves were getting choppier around the little boat.

Just as the last of the crew was pulling closed the doors, thunder and lightning roared across the darkening vista lightening up the sky. They felt the little tug rising and falling as the turbulent waters increased in intensity. Ma was in the galley trying to make a light supper but everything was slipping and sliding off the counter.

Everything not tied down, was thrown about in the small space. Glasses, plates, and cutlery were all thrown to the floor, A pot just put on the stove ended on the floor during a sudden swell, along with a bowl filled with biscuit mix she was going to have at supper. Knowing it was hopeless to try and proceed with a meal now, she apologized to the men and said she would prepare their meal as soon as things calmed down. The seasoned crew seemed unconcerned, as they went to lay down in their bunks and wait out the storm.

The rain was coming down hard, as lightening streaked across the sky. The swells rose and fell in sickening rhythm. As each crashing wave picked up the little tug and flung it back down into the turbulent water, Kaleb tried to appear calm like the older guys, but as he reached his bunk, he was white as a ghost and his hands were shaking. Each jolt of the boat caused Noah's back to arch and stretch the tight scarred skin. Water blisters broke open and he cried out in pain.

Apart from Noah's outbursts—no-one spoke—only the howling of the wind and the crack of thunder filled the air. Ma suddenly appeared in the hall. "Now boys," she soothed, "we've been in worse storms. Just stay in your bunks until it passes and then I'll make you a nice warm supper."

She went over to Noah and gently replaced his poultice. Leaning over him, she whispered that she could see the constant movement of the boat was causing extreme pain, so she had brought him a few sips of whiskey (with Pa's blessing). She helped him up a bit so he could swallow the burning liquid and told him it would help him to sleep through the worst of it. Patting him on his arm, she returned to her cabin.

"Are we going to die?" Noah asked of no-one in particular.

Edward answered, "Oh don't be daft—we'll be fine. I've been through much bigger storms than this—and a few of the older guys could tell you tales that would curl you hair!"

Noah wasn't so sure. Kaleb hadn't spoken in a bit and Noah asked if he was alright. He gritted his teeth and told him that he was OK and not to worry. But he was worried—plenty worried, but he would never admit that to Noah. Bracing themselves as best they could, they tried to keep from falling out of their bunks with each twist of the boat. As they lay there tense, their thoughts turned inward.

Kaleb thought of his Mum and wondered how his brother and sisters were doing. He did not know of their change of circumstances and so was worried they were getting enough to eat. They'd gone through some tough times since his Dad had passed…and now that he was the head of the household, he took his responsibilities very seriously. He had to stick this out for their sake. There was no other plan. At seventeen, he was still just a boy but the weight of the world was on his young shoulders.

Noah continued to slip in and out of consciousness. The whiskey had helped some but along with the on-going pain was the increasing fear. The sea, he now understood, was a very dangerous place. *God grant me the strength to get through this so I can get home and rescue my Mum*, he desperately prayed. If he only knew there would be no more rescuing…

Chapter 23

Ester ran toward the door. Pulling it open, her girls tumbled in with the doctor close behind. "Oh thank God, you've come, Doctor. Please help my baby."

The doctor put down his satchel, and picked up the child. Checking him over closely, he saw that the baby was in a fitful sleep and was very hot to touch. Although not coughing, his little chest was heaving with short, quick breaths. Listening to his lungs, the doctor seemed alarmed. Turning to the frantic mother, he said, "Ester, you must know he has the croup."

Wringing her hands together, tears streaming down her exhausted face, she replied, "Yes, yes, I was afraid he did. Can you do anything to help my baby, Doctor, please? Do you have medicine that can help him? I can pay you—I have money, please make him better."

"Dear woman, money is not the problem. The croup is deep in his chest and it is very unpredictable. I wish I had seen him sooner. I fear it might already be too late—"

"No, oh God no—don't say it. Please, there must be something you can do."

"Ester, you have already done everything right—you've used a poultice on his chest, steaming water to help his breathing, and cooling clothes to bring down his fever. But nothing seems to be working. His breathing is very labored—he can barely catch his breath—and his fever still has not broken."

As the little girls softly wept in the background, Ester pressed his little body to her breast cradling him to her. Witnessing the devastation and depth of this mother's pain, the doctor continued, "I do have some ointment that might help loosen up the tightness in his chest. It has worked in other cases such as this, but I caution you, Ester, those cases were not as severe as your son's. There are no guarantees, but if the ointment works and the fever breaks, he may have a chance. Keep doing all that you have done, apply the ointment every hour and I will be back tomorrow morning to hopefully seen an improvement. But it is in God's hands now."

As he was leaving, Ester slipped a few dollars his hands. "This is not necessary, Ester, I am pleased to help"

"Please doctor, I want to pay for my son's medicine. I thank you for coming so quickly and I pray you will see a difference tomorrow." As the doctor left, she cradled her rasping son and prayed like she'd never prayed before. "Please dear God, do not take my precious son."

She began to barter with God—please Dear Jesus, if you heal my son—I will give up… She realized that she had nothing to offer to God, except her unfailing faith in Him, and so she simply kept repeating 'please God save this little angel'.

Rubbing the cream on his chest, Ester knew it was going to be a long night. Leaving her older girls to care for the twins, she prepared for the fight of her life. Laying her son across her lap as the doctor had shown her, she began to tap his back repeatedly in a rhythmic motion. And so it began—boiling water so the steam could hopefully break up his congestion, applying cool cloths across his head, under his arms, across his chest, on his neck and between his groin…and as soon as she had finished the last cloth—the first ones were hot again.

Over and over she would continue this, and then flipping him over again to tap his back to help loosen the tightness in his chest—then repeat the whole thing again. It seemed to be a losing battle…until she remembered what her mother had done when her sister had taken ill with a high fever. The cool cloths had not worked then also, so following her mother's actions, Ester prepared a cool bath for her son, but this time she added some rubbing alcohol to the water and placed him in it.

She submerged him partially and splashed the cooling water over his scorched skin. Again, he screamed in pain but there was nothing else she could do. Then she removed him and rubbed the ointment onto his little chest. Finally, she would tap his back for several minutes and then back into the cooling bath—all the while praying for a miracle. Time lost all meaning, as the mother repeated over and over the ritual.

After several hours, Ester became aware that his little body was no longer bright red—but a healthier pink. His fever seemed to be dropping and she was able to take him out and cover him with a light cloth. He also seemed to be breathing easier. Wiping tears from her eyes and shaking the tiredness from her depleted body—she was beginning to feel real hope for the first time since yesterday.

Continuing to rub his chest with the ointment, she fell into a fitful sleep while cradling her child loosely in her arms. She awoke with a start. Looking down at her son, her heart missed a beat. There was no movement—she could hear no rasping. His body was cool—almost too cool. Oh my God—was he dead? Had he passed during the night without her even saying goodbye? *Dear Lord, I couldn't live if my child had left this world alone.*

Suddenly, her eyes focused on his chest. It was moving up and down ever so slightly. Leaning over him, she whispered his name, tapping his face lightly and moving his arms and legs gently. As his eyelids started to flutter, she fell sobbing to the floor, overcome with gratitude that the Lord had answered her prayers and spared her child.

Never before had she felt such elation—such sheer joy. Again, she humbly thanked God for His Mercy. Tears of happiness flowed as she woke the girls and shared the good news. All the commotion woke the twins and so they all danced around in joy, hugging each other and praising God for His gift to their family. Ester could not wait to show the doctor her son's transformation.

When the doctor arrived later that morning, he was not confident at what he would find as he approached their door. Before he had even finished knocking, the door was flung open and he stopped short at the scene unfolding inside. Laughing and crying at the same time, Ester pulled him into the room. There seemed to be kids everywhere—all laughing and twirling around…

As he eyes returned to Ester, he saw the reason for their gaiety…the little lad was awake and cooing, as if to join the festivities! The doctor took the boy and checked him thoroughly. He was in shock. "Well Ester, I am amazed—but it seems you have received your miracle. I was very afraid we would not be able to save the little lad. You have much to be grateful for, Dear."

"Yes I know, doctor. I will never be able to thank God enough for this, and I also thank Him for bringing Angels of Mercy like yourself to help."

Tonight in celebration, she would slaughter a pig. Although they would have a feast, Ester would be careful to save the leftovers. Her mother had taught her well and Ester was very thrifty. This pig would feed her family in many ways.

As they sat down at the dinner table and bowed their heads to give thanks for their blessings, Ester thought of the boys and hoped they were safe and eating well also. She thought of her poor friend whose misfortune had given this unexpected bounty to her family.

How was she doing? Was she speaking now or was she still locked in her silent world? She must try and find out. Visiting was out of the question, as the institution was so far away, but she would write and hope someone there would read it to her. She also hoped her friend would understand what she had written.

Chapter 24

All through the night, the little boat pitched wildly. Noah would fall into a fitful sleep—only to be jolted awake by a violent wave. Ma had come in several times during the night to change the poultice, and one time she also gave him a few more sips of whiskey. The searing pain in his back had gradually improved, although the pain was still pretty bad. It was always a relief when Ma placed a new, cooling poultice on his many blisters.

Several times Noah had to lean over to throw up in the bucket Ma had thoughtfully placed next to his bunk. He was surprised that anything remained inside of him to come out. Some of the older men were actually snoring—*how was that even possible*, he wearily thought.

Even Kaleb seemed to be sleeping through most of it, albeit uncomfortably. Why had he done this? Why had he thought he could be a fisherman? It all seemed so foolish now. He almost wished he was back in his kitchen, getting a beating from the old drunk. At least it didn't last long, as the old man usually passed out quickly. This horror, however, seemed to be never ending.

How could he come back a hero and rescue his mother if he couldn't even stand a storm at sea? Noah fell into a restless sleep depressed and feeling sorry for himself. Maybe he should get off at the next port and try to find another, less dangerous way to help his mother he thought drowsily…

Morning broke with warm sunshine bathing the deck of the tug. The surrounding water was like glass, clear and unbroken. It was as if the storm had never happened. Pa and some of the others were up early to survey the damage caused by the storm. One sail had come undone and was ripped almost to the mast.

Several containers of salt had been lost and some of the other supplies were gone as well. Thankfully the seal over the hold had held and their previous catches were safe and dry. As they continued to take inventory, Pa refused to get upset. Heading down for a long-overdue hot meal, they all assembled in the little galley.

Noah woke up feeling better. His stomach had finally settled and his back seemed to have improved a lot. He could actually sit up and move his shoulders around. Ma checked him out and said she was very happy with his progress. She cautioned him not to do anything really strenuous for a couple of days though and to just wear a light top so he wouldn't rub the healing skin. Cautiously, Noah made his way down to breakfast.

As Pa looked around the table, he saw the men were waiting anxiously for his report on the damages to the boat and what that would mean to the future of this season. Clearing his throat, Pa explained about the torn sail. He went on to say that although some of the supplies were lost, they would have enough to make it to the next port. A slight ripple of relief went around the table.

He said it might take a bit more time to get there, because they were reduced to a single useable sail, but that in the meantime—it would be business as usual. Although their meals might be a bit less filling—no-one would starve. Ma was a genius at making something out of nothing he continued and although the next few days might be harder than most, they would get through it.

He said nothing was ever fixed with a bad attitude, and that times like these are what made men out of boys. Noah felt uplifted by his speech and was once again excited to begin his apprenticeship under this incredible man who instilled such devotion in his crew. Pa finished up by saying 'no long faces'— the sun was out, they were about to fill their stomachs with the best home cooking aboard any vessel (to which Ma smiled lovingly at him)…so eat up and then we will tackle the jobs with a smile.

As they finished their breakfast and trooped upstairs, the mood of the men was upbeat.

Arriving on deck, the smiles on their faces slipped a bit when they saw what was in store for them. The deck was covered in flotsam and debris. It was slippery and dangerous and just walking about was difficult. Pa asked if Noah was sure he was OK to swab the deck. Noah quickly replied yes and grabbed a stiff broom.

"Careful boy, no need to rush—swab the deck slowly. Better to be safe than sorry." A couple of men starting sewing the torn sail, as Kaleb and Edward helped the others check the nets. Ma manned the wheel, as Pa went about helping where needed.

Although Noah would never admit it, he found pushing that broom very tiring. Just the effort to stay upright without falling in the slimy mess, was taking a toll on his slight frame. He had never been really strong like Kaleb, and the last couple of days had taken its toll. He was also careful not to do too much at once—he sure didn't want to injure his back again.

As he made his way slowly around the treacherous deck, he vowed to keep going. He could do this, he told himself. I will not give up. And so Noah continued to slowly sweep up the mess. Although Noah was forced to take several breaks, he would not allow his shortness of breath to stop him for long.

They all worked steadily for a few hours as the sun continued to rise in the sky. As the day became warmer, again the men began to shed their outer layers. Noah, having only worn a light shirt was comfortable as he was. As he continued to work though, Noah found dragging his heavy boots around to be very tiring.

They were hot and they were slowing him down, so he changed into his soft shoes and continued working. No-one noticed this, otherwise they would have cautioned him not to. The rubber boots not only protected him from the numerous sharp objects strewn around, but also provided much needed traction on the slippery deck. Unaware of the danger he was in, Noah rounded a corner just as one of the guys threw down his heavy sweater.

As Noah stepped on the corner of it, his foot slid out from under him. Grabbing frantically into thin air, Noah collided into the rigging and fell on top of a large ice pick used for hauling supplies around the deck.

Chapter 25

Everything seemed to be moving in slow motion. Suddenly, he was looking up at the sky. A gull swooped down and it seemed to be coming straight at him. Seconds later, the gull forgotten, he screamed in agony. The claw had sunk deep into his right thigh. Pandemonium erupted. Everything came to a standstill as Noah lay sprawled on the deck, howling in pain.

Ma came rushing over looking like she was about to faint. All work stopped as the men formed a circle around Noah. As his screams turned into deep moans of pain, the men looked on helplessly. Blood was gushing from his upper leg and as Noah was looking paler and paler, he suddenly passed out.

Screaming, Ma pushed towards him but was held back. "Keep her back!" Pa shouted as he leaned over Noah. Kaleb was shaking so bad, Edward had his arm around him holding him up. As Pa knelt down, he took in the situation.

Pa was horrified as he took in the scene. Never had he seen such a devastating injury. "Bring up the medicine chest and the boning knife. And bring the bottle of scotch, and you…shove a poker into the fire. Ma, get me some clean rags and a pot of boiling water. Move, move, everyone hurry up. Back up, guys, give me some room here."

The crew were softly whispering in shock, and Kaleb had begun to cry. Why had he brought Noah here? He was just a boy…Noah trusted him, looked up to him, like a brother he never had. This was his fault. How could he ever live with himself if Noah didn't make it. Over and over, Kaleb tortured himself with questions that could never be answered. Time seemed to stand still as everyone stood around helplessly watching the unfolding drama.

When everything was assembled, Pa started to wash around the wound. His worst fears were realized when he saw how deep the claw was embedded in Noah's leg. He knew as soon as he removed it, Noah could bleed to death in a matter of minutes if he couldn't cauterize the wound immediately. They were hundreds of miles from the nearest doctor, and it was up to him to take care of young Noah.

After sterilizing the hot poker with the liquor, he directed the others. "Hold him down and keep him still if he wakes up. I'm taking out the claw, but it might take some twisting."

Sobbing, Ma stood nearby holding the fresh rags. Pa grabbed the claw and tried to pull it out. It didn't move. Again he tried to pull it out, but still it did not move. Looking around at everyone watching, he knew what he was about to do would shock them…especially Ma, but he had no choice. Time was running out for young Noah.

Pa grasped the boning knife and started to loosen the flesh and muscle around the claw. He knew he might be crippling Noah for life, but there was no other way. If they didn't get the claw out and stop the bleeding, Noah would die. At one point Noah began to come around, but the intense pain made him slip back into unconsciousness once again.

Ma couldn't look as Noah's leg was sliced open. Even some of the seasoned men turned away. Kaleb fell down sobbing, his head in his hands. Pa continued to cut away at the muscle. He felt nauseous as well…but knew he had to continue.

God Almighty, he thought, *please let this work*. Nothing was happening… the claw refused to loosen. Finally pulling one last time, the claw was freed. As soon as the claw was removed, a stream of blood shot out of his leg.

Quickly, Pa shoved the red-hot poker into the wound. Noah screamed and then fell silent again. The smell of burnt flesh surrounded them, as Pa kept it firmly to the wound. Kaleb leaned over and retched as the smell filled his nostrils. The men started to back up unconsciously, as the scene in from of them was too graphic for even them. Some were praying softly, others were simply looking away.

The squirting finally stopped and Pa poured some scotch over the gaping wound. Wiping his face, Pa signaled for Ma to come. She knelt down, her body racked with silent sobs. Noah's leg was literally torn open. Although the blood had stopped shooting out, the wound was still oozing and burnt skin surrounded the gaping hole.

Ma thought she would pass out, as she carefully slathered ointment over Noah's leg. She then applied the rags and wrapped gauze around, tying up the ends to hold it in place.

As they picked up Noah gently, she insisted they put him in her bunk, which was bigger and closer to the galley. She could keep a closer eye on him there. She followed them down, ready to begin the longest night of her life.

Not knowing what to do, the men stood around in stunned silence. It had all happened so fast. Did they do something that caused this horrible accident? They racked their brains, going over everything in their minds. The mate who had just thrown his sweater down was taking it very hard. "My God, it's my fault. I threw that stupid sweater down…what was I thinking? Dear God, forgive me." One of the other men threw his arm around the stricken young man as they all headed down below deck.

All the men were silent as they met in the galley. A heavy pall hung over the group. "Now, I know this was an awful thing that happened—but it was an accident, plain and simple. No-one was to blame and I don't want no-one to feel responsible," Pa said firmly. Kaleb looked away feeling guilty, no matter what Pa said. "Noah is young and healthy, and Ma is going to take good care of him. We'll reach the next village in a couple of days and we'll get the doctor to fix him up good as new.

"Until then, we got fish waiting to be scooped up, so get a good night's sleep and we'll start again in the morning. And oh yes, it wouldn't hurt to say a prayer for our young mate here. Goodnight."

Silently, Pa was not so sure that things would go well for Noah. All he could do is what he told his crew to do, pray that God would spare Noah.

As they all silently returned to their bunks, Kaleb looked over at Noah's empty one. How could he sleep? He was supposed to take care of him. He had promised Noah's mom that he would. Would Noah be crippled—would he even survive? Could he ever forgive himself for letting Noah talk him into this ridiculous trip? Who were they kidding, they weren't fishermen—they were just boys with too much ego and not enough sense.

Heavenly Father, Kaleb prayed, let Noah live and he would promise to get him off this boat and bring him home where he belonged. Quicker than he thought possible, Kaleb fell into a fitful sleep.

Chapter 26

"It's my fault, Pa—I talked you into letting them come. I put too much pressure on the wee lad," Ma cried, distraught.

"Now Ma, you know how determined those lads were to go. If we hadn't said yes, they might have got on another boat with a captain and crew not as caring as ours. It's not your fault, luv—not at all. We've done all we can, we'll just have to wait and see."

"I couldn't lose another, Pa—it would break me," Ma tearfully confessed. All Pa could do was hold her tight. "I'll check his bandages every hour and watch he doesn't get a fever—that would be a sign of infection, right Pa?"

"Aye, that wouldn't be good, dear. If he starts to come around in the next few hours, give him a few sips of whiskey to help him sleep. The longer he sleeps, the less pain he will feel."

"We'll be able to get him to the doctor in time, won't we?" Ma asked worriedly.

"Time will tell, dear, if no infection sets in, he may have a chance."

Ma kept checking Noah through the night. He stirred a few times but never woke up. Ma wasn't sure if that was a good thing or not. The bandages had to be replaced several times, as the wound continued to leak slowly. True to her word, Ma checked him every hour through the night. Noah was unconscious the whole time. Each time Ma checked on him, she would softly kiss his cheek and say a silent prayer for him.

By early morning, she noticed a fine sheen on Noah's brow and he started to moan softly. Brushing the hair from his forehead, Ma's hand snapped back as she felt the heat. Dear God, she thought, The boy was burning up. She ran to get Pa. With Pa looking on, she removed the bandage again. Pa tried to hide his dismay.

Instead of blood leaking out of the wound, a greenish pus was beginning to ooze onto the bandage and there was a foul odor. "This is not good, Ma, infection is brewing."

Sobbing Ma cried, "What can we do—can we get to the village any quicker?"

"We're going as fast as we can."

"There must be something we can do," Ma implored. "I'll clean it more often…I'll keep it clean. That will work, right Pa?"

Pa said nothing as he turned away. Cleaning the outside of the wound wouldn't do much. It was the inside that was the problem. He couldn't bear however, to take away what little hope she had left. Noah was in God's hands now, and they would just have to wait to see what He decided to do.

Carefully, Ma wiped the puss away and sprinkled more liquor on the site, hoping to kill any germs. Crying softly, she spread more ointment on and wrapped fresh bandages around his leg. Dear God, she prayed, please don't take this child. My heart cannot stand another loss. Please have mercy, she beseeched.

Surely God would not have brought this child into her life, just to take him away. All through the next day she cleaned and dressed his wound repeatedly. She stripped him down and washed him with cool water. Noah did not wake up.

Finally, on the third day, the tiny fishing village was in sight. There was much movement on deck, as the crew prepared to dock. There had been little conversation the last few days, as everyone was solemn and worried about Noah. The guys pitched in to cover Kaleb's chores, as Kaleb had seemed to be in a fog, stumbling around and muttering to himself. He was just staring out into nothing, would not reply to anyone except for an occasional moan. There was no expression on his face except for a tear or two that slipped out unnoticed.

Pa was worried about him—he was taking this so hard. Ma tried to console him, but she was just as heartbroken as he. They could only guess the private hell Kaleb was putting himself through.

Why did this happen? Kaleb thought. Why did he let Noah talk him into this ridiculous plan? He should have known better…he should have just refused. Dear God, please heal this young boy. He's already been through such pain in his life…please help him now. Although the oozing had stopped, Noah was still running a high fever and had not woken up. His small frame was even slighter from not having eaten in days.

She had managed to get down a few sips of water, and one of the days even a bit of broth, but Noah was very near death. His leg had swollen up twice its size and everyone feared the worst. As they pulled up to the dock, Kaleb jumped out and ran up towards the village to find a doctor. The rest of the crew left the boat silently to wait onshore.

Sprinting up the hill, Kaleb prayed fervently. He prayed there would be a doctor on call…he prayed they would reach him in time…he prayed that they weren't already too late…but mostly he just prayed…

It seemed to take forever before Kaleb returned with a portly gentleman carrying a black satchel. Helping the doctor on board, Pa took him down into the galley. Kaleb paced back and forth on deck. Had they gotten Noah here in time? What were they doing down there? What was taking so long?

Kaleb felt like he was going to explode and was just about to go down when he heard voices coming up the stairs. Suddenly, Ma was at the top of the stairs followed by the doctor and Pa carrying Noah on a make-shift stretcher. Their faces were solemn as they maneuvered him onto the dock. Pa stopped to address the anxious crew.

Chapter 27

Reading the chart, the doctor shook his head. Still, he thought, this poor woman had not spoken a word. Her physical wounds were healing well, but there was no change in her demeanor. He knew the circumstances that had brought her here and felt great compassion for this frail little thing, so old beyond her years.

Conventional medicine had not worked and intensive one-on-one therapy had no effect either. She continued to stare blankly out at a world she no longer seemed to inhabit. She sat immobile all day, only eating if fed by a nurse.

The nurses reported no change. They all seemed to take a vested interest in this sad case. No signs of emotion or awareness were present and the doctor was baffled as to what more they could do for her. They had exhausted all options and he feared that this woman would remain in this catatonic state until she died. Her future seemed bleak. All they could do for her now, was to keep her comfortable and hope she would somehow break through this self-imposed silent tomb she dwelled in.

She had no visitors—no contact with the outside world. The only family she had was a son, who could not be reached. Each morning the doctor would check her chart, in hopes some progress had been made. Each morning, he was again disappointed. One day, a nurse showed the doctor a letter that had arrived addressed to her. After reading the short note, he decided this might just be the breakthrough they were hoping for.

Sitting down in front of her, he explained that a note had arrived from her friend. As he began to read the note slowly, he watched closely for any signs of recognition. There were none. Her face was a blank slate. She didn't even blink. Sighing softly, the doctor squeezed her hand and left.

Nurse Sophie was at the nurses station receiving the day shift's report. "I'm afraid there's been no change with the poor thing. The doctor even read a letter from her friend with good news about her son—but nothing."

Nurse Sophie sighed and agreed that it was a very tragic case for sure. That night was like any other. She was fed her dinner, was bathed and prepared for bed. After giving her nighttime meds, she was tucked in for the night. Her door was locked as usual and the lights turned off. Nurse Sophie reported no disturbances—no activity through the night. Everything was as it should be.

When the morning shift arrived, the nurse on-duty opened her door to get her up for the day. Dropping her keys, the young nurse ran screaming to the nurse's station. The alarm was sounded and all available staff ran to her room.

She was hanging from the overhead light. A chair lay toppled on its side. It was immediately obvious that she was dead. Shock and dismay rippled through the small group, as they surveyed the tableau around them. How was this possible? The poor woman had been, to all intents and purposes, comatose—unable to even care for her own personal needs. How could she have done this?

The doctor had been summoned, and the police called. Until they arrived, there was nothing else anyone could do. A security guard was stationed outside the door to preserve the scene. When the doctor arrived, the guard stepped aside to allow him into the room. The nurse who'd found the woman was softly crying in the corner of the room. As they waited for the police to arrive, the doctor tried to make sense of what had happened here. His mind travelled back to the day she had arrived.

The double doors had opened and two officers were escorting a young woman. The doctor looked up from the nurse's station taking in the scene. The officers were supporting her as they led her down the corridor. She was very thin, frail actually, and her face was bruised and swollen. Her nose was broken and one arm hung crookedly. Her long tangled hair hung limply about her hunched shoulders.

They propelled her along, her feet dragging behind her. It was as if she was trying to curl up and disappear. She made no sound and seemed unaware of her surroundings. As the paperwork was being completed for her admission, the doctor looked into her eyes. There was nothing there.

After reading her file, the doctor was shocked. He could not believe what this poor woman had been through in her short life. At closer inspection, the woman appeared much older than her age. The years of abuse had taken its toll on her body. Her file outlined the horrors that her husband had put her through.

Physical, emotional and sexual abuse was her life. This had been going on for years, and was witnessed by many people in her community. Why, he thought, had no-one ever stepped in to help her? His compassion for her was immediate and he secretly vowed to help her return from wherever she had escaped to in her mind.

And so began the daily sessions to try and reach her. She was completely dependent on others for all her daily needs. Her eyes were fixed, never moving, never responding to any movement or stimulus. Each day the doctor would spend time with her, one-on-one, trying to break through the haze that clouded her consciousness.

He found himself spending more and more time researching case studies trying to find alternative methods of treatment. He had done what he had never done before—become personally involved with his patient. She was with him when he awoke each morning, and with him as he retired for the night. Never before had he agonized over a patient like this. Each night he could be found in his study, reading—searching...trying to find the key that would unlock her prison. After several weeks of intense therapy, nothing had changed. She was, he thought, his biggest disappointment—his worst failure.

They tried everything to reach her. They tried music therapy, tactile stimulus, even taking her out for long walks. Nothing reached her. She was just a shell of the woman she used to be. Anger at her abuser ate away at the kind doctor until he had to deliberately tell himself to let go. He was doing all he could to bring her back to the land of the living...the rest was up to God.

Blinking rapidly to stave off tears, he returned to the scene before him. What had caused this to happen? Could he have prevented this? Had he missed a clue that might have alerted them? Had there been any change in her behavior? He paced back and forth, vilifying himself in his mind. What kind of doctor was he if he could not foresee something so drastic?

Years of schooling—years of practice, and still he could not save her. Had the break-through he hoped for occurred during the night, and she had been so scared—so disoriented that she'd taken her life? And how did she manage to do it, being so frail? Or had the mention of her son in the letter finally ripped through the veil—causing her to realize what she had done. Unable to live with the fact of her murdering her husband, had she succumbed and decided she could no longer go on? These questions would never be answered.

As the police arrived and began their investigation, the doctor walked sadly away. He would have to notify her family. Knowing they could not reach her son, they would have to send the letter of notification to the only person on record who knew her. Within days of sending her letter, Ester would receive a reply.

Chapter 28

Pa looked at his crew as they waited patiently for the news. Clearing his throat, he began, "Noah is very ill—the doctor has said he must be hospitalized immediately. Infection has set in and the lad's odds are not good."

There was an agonized sob from Ma. There was a sharp intake of breath from the crew as they moved in closer. Continuing, Pa said, "If he makes it at all, he could lose his leg. Only time will tell. We will know more in a day or two. Until then, all we can do is pray. We won't be going out to sea until we know what's happening with Noah. I'm sure you'll all agree that the fish can wait.

"This is more important than money, Noah is family—we will not leave him. Kaleb, you'll be wanting to come with us. The rest of you men take a well-earned rest. We'll let you know as soon as we hear anything."

The crew had no problem with the delay, as they had all grown quite fond of the young lad with the piercing blue eyes and infectious smile. They wandered off towards the tiny village, each praying for his full recovery.

Once Noah was admitted and settled into the hospital, he was immediately taken for tests. Kaleb sat down in the little visitor's lounge and prepared for a long night. His mind was racing, his thoughts all jumbled. Again he asked himself why he had agreed to this fool-hardy adventure. *He's like my little brother—what will I do if he loses his leg? Dear God, what will I do if he doesn't make it?* Silent sobs wracked his exhausted body, and he fell to his knees. *Dear God, spare Noah, he doesn't deserve this. Take me instead*, he pleaded. Pa was consoling Ma on the other sofa, but Kaleb was not even aware of them. He was in his own private world of pain.

Some time had passed, when Kaleb became aware of Ma and Pa sitting down beside him. They had gone for a coffee and had returned with a sandwich for him. He had not even noticed them leave. "You have to eat something son.

You've got to keep your strength up or you'll be no help for Noah if you don't," Pa said.

"That's right, dear," Ma agreed "You don't want to get sick too."

Kaleb accepted the sandwich and ate it absent-mindedly. Ma continued, "We'll stay with you, lad—we won't leave you alone. But what about his family—shouldn't you let his mother know?"

"Oh my God, his Mum. I totally forgot about that. What will I say? How do I tell a mother her only child is in hospital and is so ill that even if he makes it, he may lose his leg?"

Ma shook her head sadly and told him there was no easy way to tell such news—but that it had to be done. As Kaleb put pen to paper, he prayed for guidance. Kaleb wrote to his mother. He explained about the horrific accident, and told her that Noah was in hospital and getting the best care available. He also explained the severity of his condition and promised to write again as soon as they heard anything more. He apologized for asking this, but could she let Noah's Mum know. He brought the letter to the nurse's station and asked how he could mail it. They told him not to worry, they would make sure it went out the following day.

After what seemed like hours, the doctor returned. He looked tired and was rubbing his forehead. "We needed to cut away more of the infected part of his leg. There is a possibility we may have to amputate. We have started him on antibiotics though and if they work, we may be able to save the leg. He has lost a significant amount of muscle however, and if he gets through the next couple of days—he will need extensive therapy to walk again. He will also have a noticeable limp.

"Of course, he will have to stay in hospital for many weeks—the rehabilitation will be grueling—but he's young. I have every confidence that the lad will be able to overcome whatever lies ahead. Just pray he gets through the next few days."

Ma hugged Pa and said, "Thank God, I knew he would be alright."

Kaleb wasn't so enthusiastic. What would a 14-year-old boy with a gimpy leg do? Jobs were hard enough to come by for able-bodied men. What could he do—who would hire him like that? How would he make his way through this tough world with only one good leg?

Pa, sensing what was going through Kaleb's mind, touched his shoulder. "Kaleb, don't you worry none. I know what you're thinking. This happened on my boat—Noah will always have work with me. I would never turn my back on one of my mates—my crew is like family.

"You have both proven yourselves to me and you'll have jobs on my boat and a place at my table for as long as you want it."

Tears welled up in Kaleb's eyes as he hugged this amazing man he called Pa. Never before had he met such people—so full of love and compassion. He and Noah were very lucky indeed.

That night, they all took turns sitting with Noah. Although he did not wake up, his fever had broken and he looked comfortable. Ma and Pa took turns taking a break and they even convinced Kaleb to go down to the little cafeteria for a bite. By morning, they were anxious to hear what the doctor had to say. After examining Noah, the doctor turned to the small group. He said that the swelling had reduced and that the wound was looking better. His fever had broken and the doctor said the drugs seemed to be working.

He was confident that they would not have to amputate. He said that Noah wasn't out of the woods yet, but the signs were good that he would recover. He finished by saying that they had been very fortunate that Pa knew what to do and that he had probably saved his life. As he left the room, the doctor said he would look in on Noah later in the day.

As Ma hugged Pa, Kaleb shook his hand. "I reckon you saved Noah's life, Pa, and I will always be grateful to you. You and Ma have been like parents to us…we would never have come this far without you both. I know I speak for Noah when I say we love you like family."

Ma pulled him close for a warm hug while Pa cleared his throat and replied gruffly, "That's what you boys are to us…family, always and forever."

Chapter 29

A short while later, Noah began to stir. Kaleb excitedly jumped up. "Noah, you OK? How are you feeling…does it hurt much? You sure gave us a scare."

"Whoa, slow down there, son," Pa said chuckling. "Give him a chance to get his bearings."

Ma reached over and took his hand. "I just knew you would come back to us, Noah, our prayers have been answered," she said as she leaned over and hugged him gently.

Noah tried to sit up, but fell back crying out in pain. "What happened? Where am I? My leg—what's wrong with it?" His questions tumbled out faster than could be answered. "The pain is bad, really bad."

Kaleb pulled his chair close to the bed. "Noah, don't you remember the accident on the boat?"

Shutting his eyes in concentration, Noah replied, "I remember the deck was messy and dirty from the storm. Everyone was working to clean it up. But that's it—I don't remember anything else. What happened, Kaleb?"

"Noah, you had taken off your rubber boots because it was so hot. You put on your regular shoes and started swabbing the deck. When you turned the corner, you slipped and fell into the rigging. A large ice pick sunk into your leg and you passed out."

Noah looked shaken. "Oh my God, what happened then?"

"Pa had to dig the claw out of your leg and Ma bandaged it as best she could. During the next two days, your leg became infected. You were really sick, Noah, you almost died." Tears fell as Noah took in all that had happened.

"You gave us the biggest scare of our lives, dear," Ma said, her lips quivering. "Everyone, including all the crew prayed for your recovery." At that point, the doctor entered the room.

"Well, well—look who's awake. How are you feeling, Noah?"

"Doctor, my leg hurts bad. I can't move it much."

"Well, we can give you something for the pain son, but you won't be able to move it for a while."

"How bad is it, Doc?" Noah asked fearfully.

"Well son, we had to remove a large part of your leg because of the infection. The good news is that the antibiotics are working, so as soon as you're feeling stronger, we can start therapy to help you walk again."

Noah, visibly shaken, asked, "But I will be able to walk again, right Doctor?"

"Yes Noah. but you will have a long, hard road ahead of you, and you will have a noticeable limp."

Noah digested this news and said, "Well, that's alright. I guess I can live with that."

"That's the spirit, boy, you'll do just fine."

Kaleb was proud to see him take it like a man. *He's really growing up*, he thought.

Noah looked around the room and said, "Thank you all for your caring and support. I know I wouldn't be here without you."

Pa cleared his throat and said, "No need for thanks, son. You just hurry up and get better. We're going to miss you on the boat."

"Don't worry, Pa, I'll be back before you know it," Noah said, his old smile back in place. "I'll be up and walking in no time—just wait and see."

"Now son," the doctor cautioned, "you've been through a lot. Your body must heal. Once you're strong enough to begin therapy, you'll be looking at weeks of hard work before you are ready to leave the hospital and resume your life."

Disappointment shadowed Noah's face, his newfound energy weakening. Falling back against the pillows, he seemed defeated. "Hey kid, don't feel so bad. Think of it as a vacation," Kaleb said, trying to brighten him up. "Just think of Pa working us to the bone at sea—and remember those stormy nights when the bucket became your best friend!"

Noah wasn't having any of it. He muttered, "I'd rather be puking—than lying about."

Kaleb looked at Pa for help. "That's right, boy, if you want to come back to the boat, you must be fully recovered. And if I hear you've been giving the doctor a hard time—you'll have to answer to me," Pa said, trying to sound stern.

"Yes, and by the time you return, you'll be way overdue for one of my home-cooked meals—not that the food here isn't just fine, of course," Ma tried to laugh.

"Oh, no insult taken, Ma'am, I'm sure we'd all prefer your home cooking," the doctor said smiling. Looking at Noah, the doctor said, "You are a very lucky young man to have so much love and support. Just relax for a few days, and then we can start some exercises. You'll be up and around in no time. Now say goodbye to these nice folks and let them get back to their fishing. When they return, you'll be ready to shove off once more."

Ma was the first to throw her arms around Noah. Was it possible that his tiny frame was even smaller? How could she walk away and leave him all alone? She told him how much she would miss him and that she would pray for his recovery every day.

Noah clung to her, not wanting to see her go. Swallowing a lump in her throat, she kissed him and promised she'd be back before he knew it. Crying softly, she turned and quickly left the room before she broke down completely. Pa walked over to him and shook his hand. "I'm proud of you, son—you handled all this like a man. Hurry up and come back to us."

He too left quickly while he still had control of his emotions. Finally, Kaleb sat down next to him. No words were said, as his lips began to quiver. "It's OK, Kaleb," Noah said softly. "They'll take good care of me here,"

"It's not that, Noah—this shouldn't have happened. I should have watched over you better. I should have—"

"Now wait just a minute—I ain't no baby. I don't need 'taken care of'. Pa said this was an accident—nobody's fault, and I reckon he knows what he's talking about. Don't go blaming yourself. You're my brother—my family. I couldn't ask for anyone better. We've always been there for each other. We started this together, and we'll finish it together. I love you, Kaleb—go out and make me proud."

Kaleb hugged him tightly. "I love you too, little brother. I'll be back in a few weeks, and I expect to see you up and walking. And don't worry, Noah, I will let your Mum know that you are on the mend. See you soon." They embraced once more.

Before leaving the hospital, Kaleb stopped at the nurses station and wrote a quick note to his Mom. He told her the good news and once again asked her to relay it to Noah's mother.

As Ma and Pa arrived at the boat, the crew gathered pensively. Afraid of what they might hear, they stood quietly. Pa explained about Noah's surgery and how they had to remove part of his leg. He said that because the medicine seemed to be working, Noah would not lose his leg.

At that point, a cheer went up through the little crowd and everyone started talking at once. Pa held his hand up, quieting the group. "It's not all great news, I'm afraid." He went on to explain that Noah would have to learn to walk all over again, and that he faced weeks of grueling rehabilitation. Even after all that, Noah would have a significant limp.

The men promised they would help Noah as much as he needed when he returned. Pa smiled and said he was proud to have such good men as his crew. He instructed them to make ready to sail in the morning.

They had missed several days of crucial fishing, and would have to work hard to catch up. No- one seemed worried about the prospect of extra work though, as they went about their tasks, some even whistling under their breaths.

As Noah watched them go, he lost his false bravado. Sinking back into the bed, his lips began to quiver. *Can I really do this?* he asked himself. How will I be able to help my Mum if I can barely walk? And who will ever hire me like this…what kind of future will I have? These questions and many more tumbled through his brain, as the seriousness of his situation sank in.

Chapter 30

Ester was rocking the baby when the girls rushed in. "Ma. Ma, you got two letters," they squealed excitedly. *Two letters?* Ester thought. *What is going on?* The letter she'd gotten from Kaleb last week was the only letter she'd ever received, and now two more? "Give them here, girls, and go wash up for supper."

One letter she could see was from Kaleb again. Oh no, she prayed it wasn't bad news about Noah. The other letter was from the hospital where her friend was. Maybe the letter she sent to her had snapped her out of her 'spell'—she didn't know what else to call it. Maybe her friend was writing back, telling her about her new home.

Forgetting the letter from Kaleb for a moment, she opened the one from the hospital. She noticed it was on official letterhead. It was not from her friend. Why would they be writing to her? As she started to read, Kaleb's letter fell to the floor and she stopped rocking. Shaking, she put her son down and continued to read.

She gasped and tears sprang to her eyes as she finished reading. How could this be—Dear Lord, how could this be? She was so young. just a baby really. How could she be gone? And by her own hand? This can't be true. She was a God-fearing woman. She would never take her own life—that was a mortal sin. She obviously was not herself these past few weeks, but to do this?

Sitting there in shock, she remembered what had landed her friend in hospital to begin with. Killing her husband was breaking God's law also, even if he had been abusive. But when they had taken her away, she had been meek as a mouse. Again, she wondered how this could have happened.

For several minutes she sat there crying, reminiscing about the only real friend she'd ever had. Deep sorrow filled her heart as she thought of the horrific life her friend had been forced to endure. Dear God, she prayed, forgive her sins and have mercy on her soul. She didn't know what she was doing, she couldn't have. As the minutes ticked away, Ester heard soft cooing from her son. Absentmindedly, she picked up her son and went into the kitchen to prepare dinner, Kaleb's letter forgotten.

Chapter 31

They shoved out before dawn, anxious to get out to the fishing lanes. It would be a sunny day, The temperature had dropped a few degrees, which made it easier to work full days when it wasn't so hot and sticky. The heat always drained their energy, making them tired and sluggish before the day's work had been completed. So today would be a good day for fishing—sunny, crisp and clear. The mood was upbeat and they all chipped in to cover Noah's chores. The next few days they filled their quota's quickly and each night enjoyed a well-earned respite.

Days went by and the fishing was good. Pa was glad to see the crew happy and it almost felt like old times…almost…

It had become a ritual every night before turning in. They all gathered in the galley and said a prayer for Noah and counted down the days until they could see him again. Ma especially missed him and although she tried to keep a smile on her face, Pa had noticed her deep sorrow.

He was concerned for her, but felt helpless. He had seen the changes in her almost from the moment Noah had come into their lives. She'd always had a beautiful smile and a warm heart, but everything seemed to magnify since Noah's arrival. He'd seen her devotion to the boy—and had mixed feelings about it. On one hand he was happy to see her so fulfilled—so full of love and concern for him.

To see her deep maternal feelings be finally realized, was a blessing. But he also worried what would happen when it was time for the boy to return to his real mother and his life there. He was afraid that Ma would not be able to handle such a loss—how would he be able to help her through that? He worried that a deep sadness would envelope her soon.

Ma was beside herself. Every day she worried what was happening to Noah back in the hospital. Had his wound healed—was he making progress with his rehabilitation? She wondered how his poor mother had taken the news about his accident. She thought how awful it must be to be so far away from your son, at a time like this.

As she prayed for Noah and his mother, she realized how deep her feelings for Noah had become. She realized that although she welcomed the loving and protective feelings that welled up inside her, they came with a price. Deep love invited the possibility of deep hurt as well.

The days wondering if Noah would live—and now worrying if he would be able to walk again, had been the hardest times she'd had to endure. Her heart had been closed up for so long, thinking she would never experience the joys of motherhood—but now her heart was breaking. All she could do was trust in the Lord.

At the next port they stopped at, Ma needed some supplies from the little general store. As she was paying for her purchases, the man behind the counter asked if they had a Kaleb working on their boat. Surprised, Ma confirmed that they did indeed, have such a fellow.

Handing her a letter, he explained it had been forwarded from their little village. He went on to say that because they knew the route they would take, they decided to send it here. He had just been about to send it back, however, as it seemed as if they'd passed this stop. Thanking him, she accepted the letter and returned to the boat.

When she gave it to Kaleb, she watched him out of the corner of her eye. She hoped it would bear good news, as this poor boy already had so much on his shoulders. His reaction was intense. Kaleb cried out and fell to his knees. "Kaleb, what's wrong—my God, son, what's happened?" Ma cried as she knelt down beside the shaking boy.

"Oh my God—how can this be? What will I tell Noah?" Kaleb was rocking back and forth, as if in a trance.

"Kaleb, sit down here. Let me help you. What is it, dear?" Ma soothed as she sat him down at the table. Wordlessly, he handed her the letter. As Ma began to read the letter, her face paled and she whispered, 'Dear Lord' under her breath. As she read on, she too began to cry.

Grabbing Kaleb's hand, she sat down beside him. She understood the torment Kaleb was going through. How could you tell a 14-year-old boy, in hospital, fighting for his life, that first of all, his mother had killed his father (albeit in self-defense). Then, because of this tragedy, his mother had been placed in a mental institution.

And finally worst of all, his mother had hung herself to death and that he was now alone in the world. How would Noah react to this—how would it impact his recovery?

Hearing a commotion going on downstairs, Pa entered the galley. Shock registered on his face when he saw the pain on their faces. "What's wrong here—what's going on?"

Ma told him to take a seat, as she briefly told him what had happened. Handing him the letter, she sat back exhausted. Pa's hands shook as he read the news. For a moment, he was at a loss for words. He too was worried what effect this would have on Noah. Sitting there, each with their own thoughts, Ma started, "Kaleb dear, we will do this together. We will stay by your side and help you through this. By the time we see Noah again, he should be almost healed. The pain will be intense, but we will make sure he knows he's not alone.

"He has you, Kaleb—you're the closest thing to a big brother that he has. And now, he has Pa and me. He'll always be part of our family, now more than ever. And you too dear. We love you boys as if you were our own. We'll get him through this ordeal, don't you worry, son."

Kaleb hugged Ma, and again marveled at how lucky they had been to meet this wonderful couple. He remembered what his Mum had always said—'when one door closes—God will open a window. Do not despair, He will see you through all of life's trials and tribulations'.

Kaleb now understood what she meant. Although Noah had lost his dear mother, he now had Ma and Pa in his life. "Of course, Kaleb, he will always have a place in our home. I would be proud to call him son—and that applies to you too. From the moment you boys knocked on our door, dirty and starving, you stole our hearts."

Later that night on deck, as they gazed at the multitude of stars, Ma said, "You are a good man, Pa. Have I told you lately how much I love you?"

Pa chuckled, as he drew her to him. "Yes dear, but you can tell me again." As they hugged, he thought that Ma had finally gotten an answer to her repeated prayers for a child to love.

Meeting these boys had truly been a gift from above.

Getting ready for bed, Kaleb again wondered how to tell Noah the devastating news. How would he react? Dear Lord, how much can one young boy take? As he drifted off, Kaleb's thoughts went back in time…

"Hey Kaleb…want to race me to the fence post?"

"That wouldn't even be a fair fight," Kaleb laughed. He remembered the day he had shown Noah how to milk the cow and how scared he was that it would kick him in the face. And the day Noah collapsed in laughter when he slipped and fell into the pig pen. He thought how great it was to see a bit of happiness on his friend's face.

He knew the terrible life Noah had at home…no joy…no fun…He was usually quiet and withdrawn, so to see him animated like this was a blessing. "How are things going, Noah? Things any better at home?"

"Nah…I just try and stay out of the old drunk's way. At least I can run away from him most of the time—but Mum isn't so lucky."

"Geez, I feel so bad for you guys…wish there was something I could do to help."

"Well, it is what it is I guess. One day the old bastard will get what's coming to him."

Chapter 32

These last few weeks had not been easy, Noah thought. The pain had been at times almost unbearable, as he struggled to complete the exercises given to him. He'd had no idea it would be as difficult as this. It had been torture the first time he tried to put weight on his leg.

Then, as he began his rehab, it seemed he would never again be able to walk without dragging it behind him. The first time he saw what was left of his upper thigh, he wept. Gradually, he became accustomed to his new leg, and laughingly thought he'd never win any strong-man contests with his new physique.

He started each day with determination and grit. Slowly, he was able to put some weight on it, and he finally began to take a few steps. He never complained—at least not out loud, but he had some heated conversations in his head, and at times when the pain seared through his brain, his internal dialogue was very spicy, to say the least.

He always had a smile for the nurses and did what was asked—even if at times, his smile was more of a grimace. The doctor was very pleased with his progress and in fact told him he had never seen anything like it. He also said the nurses had nothing but praise for his hard work and pleasant demeanor. This was uplifting to hear and gave Noah even more energy to do his best.

All the nurses were great, but there was one in particular that was amazing. Rose was one of the senior nurses, having spent most of her adult life right there in the little hospital. She could tell you stories that would make you laugh and cry. She was an institution there and everyone loved and respected her.

Rose remembered the day they had brought Noah in. There didn't seem to be much hope for this young boy's survival. His leg was so swollen and misshapen that several of the younger nurses were distraught. They had never seen such horrific injuries before. Rose had accompanied Noah for his multitude of tests and into surgery.

She knew his chances were slim, but something told her this young man would make it. As he made it through each milestone, she saw what an outstanding fellow he was. So strong and brave…up for any challenge, determined to conquer it all. Her admiration for Noah grew day by day.

As Noah became more mobile, he began to visit the other patients on the floor. He found their stories captivating and at times truly moving. He started following the nurses from bed to bed during their rounds and asking questions—lots of questions. He delighted in helping them any way he could, and seemed to have an affinity for this profession.

The patients and staff were delighted with his warmth and tenderness. He seemed to genuinely care about their problems and was willing to spend time with anyone who seemed to need extra attention. It seemed only natural then, that Noah's thoughts ran to 'what if?' What if I didn't go back to the boat? What if I stayed right here? What better job could there be, than to help people get well?

Pushing these fanciful thoughts aside, he reminded himself that he could not afford to go to school—heck, he couldn't even read or write. And what about his commitment to go back and help his mother? No, he would have to go back to the fishing boat.

Pushing his dreams away, Noah anxiously searched the bay for the little tug. He couldn't wait to see Kaleb and Ma and Pa again. He had been working very hard and couldn't wait to show them how far he'd come. They would be so proud to see what he had accomplished. He barely needed a cane anymore and could walk with just a small limp. He couldn't wait to see their shocked expressions as he walked toward them.

Chapter 33

As Ester was putting the baby to bed, she remembered the letter from Kaleb. Ripping it open, she began to read. My God, she gasped, what was this? How much more could this poor lad take? On one hand, she was grateful she did not have to burden her friend with such painful news—and yet how could she possibly tell Noah about his mother's death when he was so ill? She knew she could not keep this from him, but Dear Lord, how would she do it? What words could she use to relay the tragic news?

Shaking her head, she sat down and asked God to guide her. She began by apologizing to Kaleb, for once again putting this on his shoulders. but knowing Noah could not read, there was no other way. She tried to explain as compassionately as possible what had transpired. Finally, after several attempts, she finished the sad little letter and sealed it up.

She was drained from the effort it took her to write it and prayed that God would bless Noah and help him through the pain and to face his uncertain future. As she lay her weary body down, she again gave thanks for the miracle she had received and for the blessings her family had been given.

As she tossed in bed, thoughts of little Noah alone in a hospital, in pain and facing such odds robbed her of her much needed sleep. She prayed they would be able to save his leg and that he would be able to adjust to his new life. Sighing softly, she glanced once more at her sleeping son and finally fell asleep.

Chapter 34

As the tug pulled into the bay, the men were anxious to get off and find out how Noah was doing. It had been a good run and the hull was filled with fish. Everyone was upbeat and happy. The season was going great and their pay would be good this year, even with Ma and Pa having to take 2 cuts at the end of the season to cover the repairs and supplies lost at sea.

The rest of the money would be split evenly between the men. This was unheard of in the fishing world. No other captain was as fair with their employees. And apart from being so generous, if you worked for Ma and Pa, you became their extended family.

One year they took a cut in their pay to help one of the crew. The young son of one of the men had developed a serious eye infection and was at risk of going blind. He required specialized treatment in hospital far away. Knowing the father would not be able to afford to bring his son there, Ma and Pa had quietly added money to his pay packet at the end of the season and told him not to mention it to anyone else.

They said that family was more important than anything else and that they were honored to help. Word of their generosity soon became known however and it became a fisherman's dream to work for them. Because the men were treated so fairly, few ever left their employ, so jobs on their little tug were few and far between.

Looking up at the sky, watching the clouds part and the sun begin to shine, Kaleb was not so excited about leaving the boat. How could he tell Noah all that had happened since he'd left? He wouldn't be upset that the old drunk had finally gotten what he deserved—but at his own mother's hand? And that she'd been taken away to a mental hospital—and finally, worst of all—his mother had taken her own life? How would Noah react to this tragic news—how would any 14-year-old cope—let alone someone recovering from a life-threatening situation?

God help me, Kaleb prayed as he climbed up onto the deck. As they were mooring the lines, Ma and Pa came up behind him. Pa put his arm around Kaleb's shoulder and whispered to him, "We know how scared you must be son, but we will be right there with you." Ma grasped his hand and with tears shining in her eyes, promised they would get through this together.

They hadn't said anything to the crew yet, as Pa felt Noah should hear the news first. He also didn't want a boat filled with depressed sailors—not good for morale. "Come along now, no sense putting off what must be done," Pa stated firmly. He told the crew to enjoy some well-earned free time. They would let them know how Noah was doing as soon as they found out.

Some of the men walked toward the little fishing village for lunch and a few beer, while a few stayed behind to finish up. It would take a while to unload the fish and restock the vessel, so they were in no hurry.

As the sad little trio walked towards the hospital, their steps unconsciously slowed down. No one wanted to do this. They all loved Noah and knew this would devastate him.

Chapter 35

Looking out of his window, Noah was finally rewarded for his persistence. There, just entering the bay, was the little tug. Whooping and hollering he practically ran down the corridor, his limp barely noticeable. "They're here— they're here," he chattered excitedly. "I saw them. Look out the window, they're here."

The old doctor looked up and smiled as two nurses followed Noah over to the window. "Well son," the doctor chuckled, "we know how hard you've worked for today."

"Should I meet them at the door—or no, maybe I should get back in bed and jump out at them when they come in." Noah was almost giddy with anticipation.

"I think you should sit down before you fall and break something!" Rose laughed.

"OK, OK, you're right," Noah conceded, "I don't want to undo everything I've done." Noah forced himself to sit down in a chair facing the entrance. *Boy*, he thought, *was this ever going to be good.*

Reaching the front door, Kaleb hesitated. Steeling himself for the ordeal ahead, he entered with Ma and Pa right behind him. There in the lobby, sitting up straight in a chair, was Noah looking fit as a fiddle. Unable to contain himself any longer, Noah jumped up and rushed towards them.

They watched in awe as Noah put one leg in front of the other, with only a slight limp. Beaming with pride, Noah flung himself into Ma's open arms. Laughing and crying, they all celebrated Noah's amazing accomplishment. This was not the time, Kaleb thought. Let him enjoy his moment. There would be plenty of time later to shatter Noah's world.

Noah was practically floating on air as he led them back to his room. There was so much to tell them and so much he wanted to know. How had the fishing gone—did the guys ever ask about him—was Kaleb an expert fisherman now?

On and on, the questions continued until Pa held up his hand laughing. "Whoa Noah, what about you? We want to know all about what's happened with you—and how on earth did you get back on your feet so quickly?"

Noah happily began to fill them in on all that had transpired the last few weeks. "The doc says he can't believe how fast I've healed. Says he's real proud of me."

"As we all are, dear," Ma said lovingly.

"As I started to feel better, I've been following the nurses around and meeting the other patients. It feels so good to help out, if only a little bit."

"You've come back from the brink of death, and we have God to thank for that, and your stubborn streak too, of course."

"Yeah, He must have heard all those prayers we said every night, Ma," Kaleb smiled.

"You guys prayed for me?" Noah asked surprised.

"Every night, after dinner before bed, the whole crew joined in and we prayed for your recovery."

"Wow, nobody's ever cared like that for me before except my Mum," Noah said, his eyes tearing up. "I really miss her, you know. Can't wait to see her again."

Chapter 36

Looking from one to the other, the three seemed to come to a decision. Kaleb swallowed nervously and there was a long pause. "What's the matter—why do you all look funny…did something happen to my Mum—did that old drunk hurt her again?" His voice began to rise as he sat up in bed. "I'll kill him, I swear if he's hurt her again."

"This is so hard, son—we do have some very bad news." Pa stopped and looked to Ma as he put his hand on Noah's trembling shoulder.

"Aye, remember we love you and will be right here with you," Ma soothed as she came closer to the bed. She began to softly cry and Noah frantically looked at Kaleb.

"What's going on, Kaleb, please tell me, what's wrong?" Noah begged him to explain.

As Kaleb sat down beside him, he grabbed his shaking hand and began to speak. "There's just no easy way to say this, Noah. There was another awful fight after we left—and it was the worst one yet. This time though, your Mum must have had enough, because she fought back."

Before Kaleb could continue, Noah broke in, "Well that's good, it's about time. I hoped she decked him good."

"Wait Noah," Kaleb continued, "there's more. She picked up a pot and hit him on the head—she hit him hard, Noah. He's dead, your Mum killed him."

Noah didn't respond immediately. Finally, after a minute, he said, "Well good—there's no loss there. She should have done it long ago." Noah sat back, his lips trembling.

"There's more, son," Pa said quietly, looking down at his hands—they were shaking. "The sheriff came and…"

"They didn't charge her, did they?" Noah cried. "They couldn't have. Everyone knew what a bastard he was. They didn't take her to jail, did they? I've got to get back. I've got to help her. I've got to go home."

"Noah honey, they didn't put her in jail," Ma soothed. Falling back against the pillows, Noah sighed in relief. "They didn't charge her, Noah, but your Mum wasn't well—you know, in her head," Ma continued cautiously. "You know she would never have done this if she was thinking right. She apparently just sat there staring off into space. She couldn't talk—she didn't respond to anything. They couldn't just leave her like that, so they put her in a hospital—one where they deal with that kind of thing," she finished.

"Well OK, I've got to go see her. I can help her. I'll be able to get through to her—she'll remember me."

Ma looked helplessly at Kaleb, silently begging him to continue. "Noah, your Ma was very sick—she wasn't herself. She didn't know what she was doing—she just snapped. You know she was a God-fearing woman so she never would have done what she did if she was in her right mind."

"Done what, Kaleb? For God's sake, what did she do?"

"Noah," Kaleb said in a rush, squeezing his hands tightly, "she killed herself—your Mum is dead."

You could see the color drain from Noah's face. Tears were streaming down, his lips moving but no sounds were coming out. Ma moved in and started to rock him back and forth. As their tears mingled, her arms tightened around his shaking frame as she soothed him the best she could.

"It's alright, Noah, your Ma's in Heaven now—no more pain. She'll never be hurt again. We're here for you dear, we won't leave you. There, there it's alright to cry." Ma continued to rock him back and forth as if he was a small child.

Noah was having a hard time breathing, as his body continued to shake. Ma told Kaleb to get the doctor. Having quickly explained what happened, the doctor gave him something to calm his nerves and quiet the racking sobs. His eyes were full of sorrow for the young boy's plight.

Pa stood back nervously. Not knowing what to do, he let Ma mother the boy. Kaleb stood back helplessly as well. After a few minutes, Noah began to quiet, as the medication began to kick in. Noah pulled back from Ma, his face wet with tears. "What about the funeral—I have to be there for that."

"Son, this happened several days ago. It's all been done. There isn't anything left for you to do," Pa said quietly.

"But what will I do—where will I go?" Noah cried plaintively.

"You'll stay with us, lad. We're your family now," Pa said firmly. "When you're well enough to return to the boat, you'll finish the season, and then move in with us after. I know that will make Ma happy, and I'm sure your Mum would have been pleased as well."

Noah couldn't make sense of all this. It was too overwhelming. So many questions—so many decisions. "It's all too much—I have to think. Can you just all go away and leave me alone for a little while? I have to make things right in my mind, OK?" Noah beseeched them.

Ma stood up and gave him a final hug. Pa shook his hand, trying to clear the lump in his throat. As Kaleb stood and hugged him, he said, "You know you're not alone right? You're like my little brother—you know I'll always be here for you." Noah nodded absently, his thoughts elsewhere. Sighing, Kaleb left the room.

They met with the doctor who assured them that this would not affect his recovery—in fact, he was almost ready to leave. He assured them that he would keep a close eye on him and that everyone loved him there, so he would be well cared for. As they walked back to the boat they were silent, each alone with their thoughts. Reaching the tug, they descended into the galley. As it was getting dark, the crew began returning to the boat.

Pa assembled the men and cleared his throat. He began by telling the them how well Noah was doing. He was strong and walking with barely a limp. He might even be ready to return to the boat. He paused for a moment as the men all smiled and congratulated one another.

Holding up his hand for silence, he continued, "I'm afraid there's been some very bad news as well, men. We have just learned that his mother has died, and that Noah is now alone in the world." The men were in a state of shock when they heard the news. No-one knew what to say. Pa did not go into specifics, thinking Noah could choose when and what to share with them. "Ma and I have assured Noah he will always be a part of our family and I know you men will do your part in welcoming him back."

Ma started fussing around the kitchen, as Pa sank heavily into a chair. Kaleb was at a loss—he didn't know what to do. He went to his bunk and laid down looking up at the ceiling. How was Noah going to deal with this loss? He was just a boy, for God's sake. Sure, Noah had taken the news about his leg like a man—but this? This was too much.

He thought how he would handle such news. If suddenly, in an instant—you're all alone in the world. Suddenly no family—no home to return to. Sure it was grand that Ma and Pa would take Noah in—but that could never ease the pain of losing your own Mum.

Dear Lord, Ma thought, as she puttered around trying to keep busy. I know I've always prayed to have a child—but not like this. That poor boy. How could he possibly handle this? How could she help him through this tragedy? She prayed for guidance as she began to make the evening meal.

As Pa filled his pipe and went up on deck, he thought how much this young lad was being tested. Having to grow up in an abusive household, then having his terrible accident- and now this. His childhood firmly behind him, he must now become a man. Pa felt saddened and helpless. As Pa joined the men downstairs for a light supper they all ate in silence and went to bed early. No-one felt like doing anything else, as the mood on the little tug was solemn.

Chapter 37

Noah lay very still, as memories flooded his brain. Most of them were not good. All the fights, all the times he'd seen his mother bleeding and crying. The times he'd wished he had killed the old man—all came rushing back. As the memories swirled around in his head, his hands clenched into fists. Tears of frustration fell silently and soaked his shirt as the violent memories continued.

Why hadn't he done something—why hadn't he helped her? What kind of son could walk out and leave his mom alone with that monster? As he realized the brutal life his mom had lived, he felt ashamed and deeply saddened for not being able to keep her safe. He would live with regret for the rest of his life. As he wept, the pictures in his mind began to change.

He blinked as his mother's smiling face came into view. She was happy— she was content. She seemed to be almost glowing and her face appeared to be years younger. The lines and creases brought on from constant stress had melted away and he saw what she must have looked like in her youth. She was beautiful.

He remembered the day Ma had woken him up with a gentle kiss on his cheek. "Happy Birthday, son," she whispered into his ear, as she slipped a few coins into his hand. Where she had gotten the change he never knew, but the memory was sweet and clear. He remembered the first day he left for school— how she had hugged him tight, not wanting to let him go.

"Don't baby the boy," the old drunk had yelled "He's just going to school—and what a waste of time that will be too." As it turned out, he was yanked out before he even learned to read and write. The chores around the farm were far more important, the old man decreed.

Noah remembered when he was sick and feverish. Every time he awoke, his Mum was there gently wiping his brow. He recalled the day he helped his mother bake cookies. How the flour had spilled and covered everything. The little kitchen had looked like a cyclone had went through it and Ma just laughed and said she hoped he wouldn't decide to become a baker. How the old drunk had come home and screamed at her to stop making the boy a "sissy." She just winked at Noah and shooed him out of the room.

As these bittersweet memories continued, Noah's hands relaxed and his tears began to slow. A feeling of acceptance came over him. Again he saw his mother's smiling face and a wave of peace engulfed him. He understood. He realized that she was in a better place—that she was happy and wanted him to go on with his life, and not to be sad. He knew in his heart that he would see her again and until that day, he must do all he could to make her proud.

He remembered what Ma and Pa had said—their loving faces full of concern for him. How they assured him he would always be welcomed in their home, that he would be like their own son. He thought of Kaleb, as close as any blood-brother could be, and knew he would get through this. But there was still much to think about—decisions to be made.

Chapter 38

As they once again walked towards the hospital, the three were uncertain as to what Noah had decided to do. The boat was empty of its cargo, cleaned, stocked and ready to go. They just had to get their last mate. Opening the front door, they saw Noah waiting for them in the lobby. He was dressed and sat patiently. There appeared to be something different about him. Not so much in his appearance but in his demeanor.

He seemed relaxed—in control of the situation. Older than his 14 years. It was if he had grown up overnight. As they approached him, a hint of a smile touched his lips. He stood up and accepted Ma's hug. As they all sat down, Noah began…

"First, I want to thank you all for your compassion and concern for me. I know how hard it must have been for you to tell me this terrible news—almost as hard as it was for me to hear it. It was very difficult at first, I won't lie. I wanted to scream—to break something. I couldn't control my tears as I realized how I had failed my Mum—how this was all my fault. Feelings of self-hatred and blame filled my heart and I thought I couldn't go on."

As Ma started to get up, Noah held up his hand. "No Ma, let me continue." Sniffing softly, Ma sat back down and grabbed Pa's hand. "I thought I'd felt the worst pain in my life when my leg was healing—but this was much worse. The pain I felt in my leg was physical -this pain was in my heart. It was so real and so excruciating, at one point I actually thought I was having a heart attack.

"I now know what they mean when they say 'someone died of a broken heart'—I almost did. But then something extraordinary happened…I saw my mother…I actually saw her. She was smiling and happy and at peace. She came to me to let me know that she was alright and that I must go on with my life."

Tears were now flowing down Ma's face, as she listened to this young lad so wise beyond his years. "Well, that's just fine," Pa said gruffly. "You'll be coming with us now then."

Noah shook his head slowly. "No Pa, I've had a change of heart. I've done some real soul-searching. These last few weeks have really changed me. I saw what working in a hospital is all about. I saw what a difference someone can make in a person's life. It was truly awe-inspiring. I watched as doctors and nurses helped their patients, not just physically—but emotionally as well.

"It made me rethink my whole future. I felt a calling—I felt like this was what I was supposed to do with my life. But I knew I couldn't, because of my commitment to my Mum. I knew I must return home to help financially and most importantly to keep her safe. Now circumstances are such, that I no longer have any reason to go home."

Ma looked at Pa with uncertainty. *What was he saying?* she thought. Noah continued, "I think my Mum would want me to do what feels right. This feels right to me. I know I will never be a doctor or a nurse—heck, I can't even read or write, but I just know I'm meant to be here to help in any way I can."

"But Noah, how will you live—where will you stay?" Kaleb asked worriedly.

"That's the best part," Noah said excitedly, his old enthusiasm returning. "The farm wasn't worth much, but it will give me a bit to start out with, and the Doctor has agreed to let me use a small cot in a back room, He's even agreed to pay me a small wage for helping around here. I don't need much, just to be able to watch and learn and help folks is more than enough—that will be the best reward."

Ma looked at Pa. His face seemed to age a bit in the last few minutes. Ma sighed as she stood up. "Well, it looks like you've thought things out pretty good, son," Pa said hesitantly.

"Oh Noah, I'm going to miss you so much," Ma choked as she pulled him to her.

"You know where I am—I expect you to visit every time you dock here. Even though I never had a father and have just lost my Mum—God has blessed me by giving me a new loving family. I love you both very much," Noah replied, his voice cracking with emotion.

Pa shook his hand and said, "I'm proud of you, son—you've become a man before our very eyes." As he turned to go, he wiped his nose with his handkerchief.

"I love you too, Noah. You are the son I never had. I will pray for you every night and ask that your dreams come true," Ma said as she hugged him one last time.

Noah held on for a moment, not wanting to let her go. *Am I making the right choice here?* he asked himself. His eyes were bright with unshed tears. Could he really let these wonderful people walk out of his life like this? Although this was the hardest decision he'd ever made in his young life, he knew—he felt in his heart that it was the right one.

As Kaleb stood up, Noah held out his hand. Brushing it aside, Kaleb wrapped his arms around him. "I'll be checking on you, little brother—so be good. It won't be the same without you, Noah. I will miss you too so much. I never had a friend like you before—and I don't think I ever will again." Kaleb squeezed him tightly.

"Hey, don't be getting all mushy with me now, I ain't dying you know, just changing careers." Noah tried to make light of the situation before he completely fell apart. Walking away slowly, Kaleb thought something had indeed died—an innocence they had shared. That special bond between them would never be quite the same.

Chapter 39

It was almost midnight—his shift was over. By the looks of the weather though, he'd probably be asked to stay on. New York City seemed to produce a multitude of patients on nights like this. It was cold and rainy, the roads were wet and slick. Accidents seemed to double and the injured would begin to pile up. They also saw an increase in stabbings and muggings.

Domestic disputes and attempted suicides also seemed to increase with this depressing weather as well.

Sighing, he looked over the board of people yet to be seen. They were pretty much up-to-date. He could slip out now—he had officially ended his shift. He would stick around for a few more minutes though, in case a flurry of patients came in.

He'd been around for almost 2 years now, but he still felt like an outsider. It was probably his own fault, he thought, as he was not much of a 'joiner'. He usually kept to himself and declined most invitations from fellow staff. His priorities were his patients and most of his time and energy went to them. Keeping up with the mountain of reading regarding new procedures and safety measures filled most of what was left in his day.

Although he was well-liked and respected by his peers, he had gotten a reputation for being unapproachable with regards to any after-hours activities. It wasn't so much that he was anti-social, just that he never seemed to have time for social activities.

He'd had a couple of girlfriends over the years, but there was only one who stayed in his mind and in his heart. Up until Katie came into his life, he wasn't ready for any long term commitments. His work was his first priority.

From the very beginning when Noah realized his true calling, he was devoted to becoming the best care-giver possible. It wasn't until later that his path had brought him to med school and beyond.

His patients loved him, not only because of his skill as a physician, but because he really seemed to care. He would go out of his way to help them in any way he could. Sometimes, because of this, he was admonished by his supervisor for becoming too involved with his patient's lives. Just heal them and send them on their way, he was told. You're their doctor—not their confessor.

He still wrestled with this concept however, as Noah felt emotional wellness went hand-in-hand with physical well-being. As he tried to convey how responsible he would feel if something happened because he hadn't followed through, his supervisor just smiled as he walked away shaking his head.

He was just a rookie, he thought. Fresh out of med school, head filled with lofty notions of 'saving' the world. Give him a few years in the trenches and he would come back to reality. He too had once felt like Noah, full of energy and optimism, but time and the cold realties of daily life in the ER had stripped him of his youthful intentions. He would never let Noah go however, as he was one of his best doctors and they were short of staff to begin with. Who was he to tell him how to live his life?

He would not be the one to dash his dreams and break his spirit. If he wanted to devote every spare moment to their personal problems, that was his decision. As long as it didn't interfere with his ability to do his job, he would stay out of it.

Deciding there wasn't going to be an emergency any time soon, Noah got his things together and stepped out into the early morning rain. As he walked in the downpour, he pulled his collar closer against the damp, bone-chilling cold. His small apartment was only a couple of blocks away. He had chosen it for that reason. It was tiny and pretty sparse. There were no homey touches, no comfortable couches or rugs. Just the bare-bones…just the bare minimum. It wasn't meant to be a retreat…simply a place to eat and sleep.

Unlocking his door, he shook the water from his coat and placed his sodden shoes on the grate. Entering his small kitchen, he brewed some strong coffee. He probably had another couple of hours of paperwork to do before he could rest. Making a ham and cheese sandwich, he sat down at the little table to eat his over-due supper.

Wiping the tiredness from his eyes, he began his studies. Sometime later, exhausted, he closed his books. Too tired to shower, he removed his shirt, unbuckled his pants, and fell into bed. He slept.

Chapter 40

In his dreams, Noah remembered the first time he saw Katie. He was walking down the hallway at his post grad school after graduating from medical school the year before. Something caught his eye and as he turned his head, there she was. She was obviously sharing a joke with a fellow student and her laughter rang out.

Her long blonde hair was tied up in a bow and she was simply the prettiest girl he'd ever seen. His heart actually skipped a beat. Who was this vision? he asked himself. As she went to class, he followed at a distance. What is wrong with me? He had never felt this compulsion before. He felt a bit like a stalker but couldn't help himself.

As he rounded the corner, he saw her slip into the classroom. Trying to walk nonchalantly by, he saw it was a psychology class. Because of his long-time interest in patients mental as well as physical health, he was even more intrigued. As he continued to his class, Katie remained in his thoughts.

They were sitting in the coffee shop and Noah knew he had to go over and introduce himself. Feeling like a silly teenager again he stepped up to their table. Their conversation paused as Katie looked up at him. Suddenly tongue-tied, he fumbled with his words. "Hi there, my name is Noah and I saw you in the hall the other day. I saw you go into a psych class and I've always been interested in a patient's mental health as well as their physical well-being. Oh, did I say I'm in pre-med…anyway, I thought it would be nice to meet you," Noah finished, feeling ridiculous.

"Oh really," Katie said amused. "That's nice. Would you like to join us?"

Grinning from ear to ear, Noah happily sat down. And so began their love affair.

Chapter 41

It wasn't long until they moved in with each other. They had found a tiny apartment off campus and were deliriously happy. They spent each night cuddled on their pull-out couch and spent hours telling their life's stories to each other. Katie was shocked at what Noah had gone through so early in his life. She had nothing so dramatic about herself to share with Noah.

She was an only child (like Noah) but that was where the similarities ended. She came from a wealthy family and never had to work for anything in her life. You would think she'd be spoiled and entitled but she was just the opposite. Her comfortable upbringing only made her more compassionate for those less fortunate. Her goal was to become a psychologist and treat teenagers at risk.

Mental health was rampart and if it wasn't misdiagnosed, it went unreported. She wanted to de- stigmatize the issue and make it more comfortable for young people to come in for help. Noah was amazed at how they had chosen similar paths. He explained he had always felt mental wellness went hand in hand with physical well-being too.

They had been dating all semester and things couldn't have been better. They were so alike in so many ways. Katie had a natural love of people and like Noah, never tired of lending an ear to someone in need. He remembered how much fun they had searching the little antique shops for 'treasures' for their little apartment (it didn't take much, as it was so small). The day they had hung curtains (twice—as the first time had been crooked, Katie said) and finally just collapsed in giggles on their couch, eating pizza left over from the night before.

Noah had been waiting for some time now at the little restaurant they had made plans to meet after their last class. Checking his watch and looking out the window at the sun quickly setting, he made a decision. He would retrace her steps and find her…as something must be wrong. She had always at least called if she was going to be late.

Frantically, Noah sprinted through the campus looking for her. He talked to many of her friends but no-one had seen her. Katie was nowhere to be found. it was now very late and he was desperate. The only other thing he could do was to check the local hospital. Running through the front doors, Noah went straight to the front desk.

Noah was distraught, barely able to give a description of Katie. The in-take nurse assured him that no-one by that name had been admitted. She said they had only one admission a couple of hours ago, and that had been a young girl who was suicidal. Turning to go, an idea came to him. "What room is she in?"

"Well, I'm sorry, sir, but unless you are family we are unable to give that information." The nurse could see that this man was at his wit's end and felt bad for him.

"Did this girl come in with anyone…the young woman I described?"

"I'm sorry Sir, I was not at that desk then, but if you wait just a moment, I will ask the nurse that was."

Thanking her, Noah paced back and forth nervously. A few minutes later (felt like a few hours) the nurse returned. "It appears she did accompany the teen, so I guess it would be alright to let her know you are in the waiting room. I'm sure your friend will come out to talk with you." Gratefully, Noah thanked her.

As Katie came rushing down the corridor, Noah scooped her up. "Oh my God, I was so worried."

"I'm sorry, honey. I was so caught up with what was happening, I totally forgot to call you."

"What's going on, Katie—what happened?"

"Here, let's sit down and I'll explain." As they sat down in a corner of the waiting room, Katie grabbed his hands. "I can talk for a bit now because they have the poor girl sedated. I was walking towards the restaurant, when I heard soft weeping. As I looked around to see where it was coming from, I saw a small dark figure huddling on the ground beneath a tree. I went over to see if I could help.

"It was a young girl, Noah, she was barely 16 years old. She just kept saying 'I couldn't do it, I couldn't do it'. As I sat down beside her, she looked up from eyes brimming with tears. 'I couldn't do it,' she replied sorrowfully. 'I can't even get that right,' she spat out.

"Taking her hands in mine, I ask her what was wrong…could I help. She said bitterly, 'No-one can help—no-one cares.' Pulling her to me, I rubbed her back telling her that I cared very much. She replied, 'Why would you care—you don't even know me?'

"'You don't need to know someone, honey, to feel compassion.' Her sobs slowly eased and she quieted down. She began to tell me her sad little story."

Chapter 42

She had been orphaned since she was 12 and as there was no other family, she was placed into foster care. The foster care system tries to do their best for their wards, but good families were few and far between. The first family she was placed with was pretty good. She had her own room and the rules were easy to follow. She felt she could get through this tragic time, here with this family. But it didn't last.

The foster-mom got sick and they had to move her to another family, just after her 13th birthday. This one was not like the first one at all. There were 3 girls and two boys, and she made the sixth. The 4 girls shared one room, while the boys had the other room. It was obvious from the beginning that this family was in it only for the money. There were no family dinners, you just grabbed whatever you could—whenever you could.

The foster mom would say, "I ain't your mom and I sure as hell ain't your babysitter. You want something…get it yourself and you better make damn sure you clean up after yourself." The other girls were pretty tough, and as she was low-man on the totem pole, she only got the scraps that were left.

But the boys were the real problem. They would leer at the girls whenever they left their room, laughing and speaking dirty to them. I guess that other girls were used to it, but she lived in constant fear. They say animals can smell fear off humans—and these boys were animals. They seemed to focus all their attention on her and one time they grabbed her and pushed her against the wall, rubbing their filthy hands all over her quivering body, She ran away that night.

Third time's the charm—right? Wrong. When they caught her, they placed her with a third family. She was by this time so traumatized that she couldn't let her guard down. She did what she was told and kept quiet. Her grades were slipping dramatically, but she just didn't care—neither did anyone else. It was a bleak existence.

The mother did try, at least she made supper, but apart from food, she had nothing else to give the child. There was no warmth, no bonding. The husband was an old drunk and from the moment he came home from work, until it was time for bed, he simply sat in his recliner throwing back beers. The wife even brought his meals on a TV tray so he wouldn't have to move for that. She often wondered how and when he went to the bathroom—but decided she really didn't want to know.

Several months passed uneventfully. Then one day the door opened and there was a young man about 17 standing there. He looked mean and dangerous, with a cigarette hanging out of his mouth and a sneer on his face. Her blood ran cold. The woman came running out of the kitchen, throwing her arms around him.

Well, I guess she does have feelings after all, the girl thought. The whole time the woman was hugging her son, his steely eyes travelled up and down her body. The old man actually got up from his chair and greeted him, not however with the same welcome the mom had given him. "Well, they finally let you out—guess they couldn't put up with you either."

"Don't worry, old man, I ain't staying long in this dump. Just getting a few things, but hey, looks like you've got yourself a new toy…have you played with it yet?" he sneered. The girl ran away that night.

Now considered a habitual runaway…it was even harder to find a family who would take her. They finally found one. A mother and her 17-year-old daughter would accept her. She finally thought she could exist there as there was no man around to be a threat.

Again, she was misguided. The mother was aloof and very clearly partial to her daughter. The daughter was spoiled rotten and had a mean streak. She complained about everything and made fun of anything the young girl did. She was now almost 16 and would soon age out of the system.

From the minute she arrived, she was made to do all the chores around the house…everything.

From the moment she woke up until she fell exhausted into her tiny cot, they worked her to the bone. The woman pulled her out of school saying she had no time for such things, as she would never make it in the world. She was too stupid—only fit for cleaning and cooking. She said she was actually doing her a favor, teaching her skills she could actually use later on in life.

She had become a real-life Cinderella…but there would be no Fairy Godmother and no Prince to twirl her around at the ball. She tried to keep up, she really tried. But day by day, she became sadder and sadder. *Why do I even bother—they're right. I have no future, no-one will ever want me, look at me, I'm disgusting, stupid just like they said. Nobody loves me—nobody cares.* Finally she could take no more.

Taking a knife from the kitchen, she quietly slipped out the back door. She wandered for miles sobbing, clutching the knife. People would glance her way then look away. 'They don't care about me—nobody does.' These negative thoughts kept swirling around in her young mind. Exhausted, she finally dropped down next to a tree and contemplated what she was about to do. Vaguely, she remembered a Bible class from long ago talking about taking your own life and that it was a sin. But surely God would understand the horrors she been through and would forgive her.

Her mind set, she positioned the knife over her wrist. Several times she tried to cut, actually breaking the skin once, but it was only a scratch. Throwing down the knife, she started to cry softly, almost spent. She kept repeating how useless she was—how she couldn't even kill herself. "That's how I found her, Noah. I finally convinced her to go to the hospital but she would agree only if I went with her."

Chapter 43

Holding Katie tightly, Noah was shocked into silence for a moment. "That poor girl. Thank God you found her, she may have tried another way to end her life. My heart breaks for these kids who have nowhere to go and no-one who cares if they live or die."

"I knew you would understand, Noah, that's why I love you so much. I want to stay with her until she wakes up.

"I've been busy while she's been sedated. I've phoned around and one call led to another, and as my contacts heard her tragic tale they all were touched. Finally I was told about a place that might be perfect for the young girl. This elderly couple is alone, their children living many hours away. Two fill their empty nest and feel needed again they had been volunteering at homeless shelters. When they heard about this girl, they immediately felt a connection.

"They are willing to bring her into their home and care for her as if she was family. I'm so excited to tell her. I may have just changed her live, maybe even saved her life!" Katie was glowing with happiness.

It had been several weeks since she'd found the home for the young girl. She had kept in touch and learned that she was flourishing. She had gone back to school and her grades were improving and the old couple just loved her. That amazing experience was so powerful, that an idea had formed in Katie's mind. After mulling it around for a few days, she decided to get Noah's input.

"I've been thinking about that girl and how I was able to help her. I've never felt so fulfilled, Noah. I've always felt the need to make a difference in this world, and I think I know how to do that now. I want to talk to my parents and see if they would be willing to start a foundation that would fund a home for homeless teens.

"It wouldn't be anything like a homeless shelter…it would be an actual home, with separate bedrooms, living and rec rooms and a large eat-in kitchen. There would be round the clock supervision and I would be one of the phycologists on-site. Whether they just needed to talk or had real mental problems, I would be there for them.

" They would have rules and guidelines (as teens crave structure) and would earn privileges such as staying up late, radios in the rooms (as long as they didn't abuse it) and such. They would have to do well in school, help around the house (no Cinderella abuse!) and help in the kitchen.

"It has been proven that if children help prepare a meal, they will be more prone to eat it. I'm sure that probably applies to teenagers too." Catching her breath, Katie looked to Noah to see his reaction.

Stunned, he simply picked her up and swung Katie around. "You are a treasure! What a beautiful heart you have. I'm sure your parents would be proud to help in any way. I am so lucky to have found you." Laughing, Katie kissed him fervently.

Who knew setting up a foundation would involve so much work—so much planning. The easiest part was getting the initial funding from Katie's parents. They glowed with pride when Katie explained what she wanted to do. Finding a house to suit was a different matter. This pilot project was to have 6 bedrooms…and would accommodate 5 girls and one 'house mother'.

It had to be close to the high school (but not too close) and it had to have a large fenced in backyard so the girls would feel safe. But the real problem was finding this house in the right zoning area. Because it was being used to hold students, not just a family, the area had to be zoned for commercial use.

After much searching, a suitable house was found. It was an older home that offered large airy rooms and had a wrap-around porch. The backyard was fenced in and offered several shade trees where the girls could sit out and still have their space. Katie did not want to be the one to pick which girls would live there, saying that would be too hard on her tender heart. A 3-person committee had been set up to oversee the day to day running of home, and they would determine which girls would be chosen from a list sent over by Children's Services.

"They were set to open the week following Thanksgiving, Katie said, so that these girls could have possibly their first real Christmas in their lives.

Thanksgiving was next weekend and Katie had invited Noah home for the holidays. Her parents were excited to finally meet this dashing young doctor-to-be (at least that's what Katie told him). Like himself, Katie was an only child and was the apple of her parents eyes. Noah was planning a big surprise for Katie during their visit. He had felt it was time to make things official and had bought a ring. He spent considerable time picking it out. It had to be just right.

He knew she wouldn't want anything big and flashy…that wasn't her. But he wanted it to be special. He finally found the perfect ring at an antique store. It was a small heart-shaped diamond, surrounded by sparkling rubies. He knew it would signify her heart that she shared with everyone. He couldn't wait to get down on one knee.

Chapter 44

By mid-day, he was up again and reading the latest publications on lowering infections in emergency rooms. He felt very strongly that better hygiene could save lives. Putting down the papers, he showered and made some lunch. This would probably be the last meal he would have for a while as his next shift started soon. The weather had cleared and as he walked to the hospital he was optimistic that he would have a quiet shift.

Walking through the front doors, he immediately knew he'd been wrong. The waiting room was filled with sick, restless patients and the board inside the emergency room was already overloaded. "Noah, sure glad to see you, man—it's a zoo in here," a colleague said, clapping him on his back.

"What's going on?"

"Well, there were a couple of accidents, back-to-back come in, the roads being so slick and all, but the majority of the people are displaying signs of a nasty bug that must be going around. It seems to infect everyone it comes in contact with."

"Are we instigating protocol with regards to infectious diseases?" Noah asked as he stepped into a gown and grabbed a mask.

"Yeah, yeah Noah, we're washing our hands and wearing gloves."

"But what about masks and changing gowns from room-to-room?"

"We don't have time for that, kid, grab a chart and follow me." Shaking his head in disbelief, Noah follow him through the congested corridor. Everywhere he looked, there were sick, coughing people. They lay on stretchers in the hallway, those that could stand were leaning against the wall for support and there were even a few stretched out the floor. The sounds of people moaning and children crying filled his ears and the pervasive smells of incontinence and vomit assaulted his senses.

He was shocked—he'd never witnessed such devastation before. It looked like a war-zone.

They entered an examining room where a young man (boy really) was coughing and spitting up blood. "How long have you been like this, son?" Noah asked, full of concern.

"It started a couple of days ago—but I only started coughing up blood today," the boy said between spasms.

Turning to the nurse, Noah asked for blood tests and a chest x-ray. "You're running a very high fever and your lungs are very congested, Mr....."

"Shane, just call me Shane, Doc. Yeah, I don't feel so good."

"Is there anyone else in your family that's sick, Shane?"

"Well, my mother has passed and my little sister is staying with my Auntie while my Dad is out of town."

"What does your Dad do, Shane, that takes him out of the city?"

"He is a distributor of seafood for the whole North East," Shane said proudly. "He travels up and down the coast, supplying restaurants and such. Once a month he does his rounds. He's usually gone about 5 days."

"Well, when he returns—make sure he comes in for a blood test. Your sister and Aunty must be checked also. It looks like you might have an aggressive strain of bacteria that could turn into pneumonia. The tests will confirm this I believe. We'll keep you here a few days and monitor how the antibiotics are working. If you respond well, you'll be able to go home then."

"I'll phone Auntie and tell her to bring Lily to her doctor. I'm not sure when my Dad will be back, but I will keep trying him at home."

"Good boy," Noah said, "but after that, lie back and try to rest. We'll get you a room as soon as possible. Let me know what's happening with your family Shane. If they begin to show symptoms, they will need to be hospitalized also. I'll check back with you later, son."

"Is it really serious, Doc, could we die?"

"If we catch it in time, the medication should be able to clear it. If it turns into pneumonia however, that is a possibility. But we won't think like that, right?"

"Right Doc. Thanks for being so nice. Some doctors have you in and out before you know it."

Not wanting to talk ill of his peers, Noah just smiled and said, "Sometimes we just don't have enough time to spend with all our patients. We try our best, but when the waiting rooms are overflowing, it gets pretty hard."

"I understand Doc, I didn't mean anything bad by it," Shane said, looking contrite.

"It's OK, we all get frustrated. Just let me know when your family reports in." Stepping out of the room, Noah threw his mask and gown into the laundry bag outside the room. He stripped off his gloves and washed his hands thoroughly. He was adamant that these precautions be taken to stop any infection from sweeping through the hospital. He had preached relentlessly to his colleagues and had swayed most of them. There were still a few, however, who felt gloves and hand washing was sufficient.

Replacing his gown, Noah stepped into the next cubicle. There was an old man coughing and having trouble breathing. As Noah checked him, he felt sorry for him, as he looked like a transient. When he looked at his chart, he thought the man looked far older than his true age. "How are you doing, sir, how long have you been sick like this?"

"This is the third day," the old man rasped.

"Well, we'll just get you started on some oxygen to help you breath and then we'll draw some blood to see what the problem is, OK?"

"Thank you, son," he whispered.

"Do you have any family we could call for you?"

"No, been on my own most of my life"

"OK then, you just relax and we'll take it from here." As Noah left the room, he ordered blood tests and continued monitoring.

As Noah continued his shift, his thoughts returned to the old man. Checking his chart again, he saw that he did indeed have the virus. Knowing at his age, this could prove to be very serious he returned to his room. He was not doing well. It had been determined that he also suffered from a blood infection which would only complicate things further. The old man was barely coherent, muttering something softly.

As Noah leaned closer to try and decipher what he was trying to say, he thought he heard him whisper "my love, my love". Noah took the oxygen mask off for a minute to try and get him to clarify, but to no avail. He slipped into a coma.

Sighing, Noah stepped out and changed gowns again. As the day progressed, he kept thinking of the old man. Passing a fellow doctor in the hall, he asked for his input on how to best treat him. He was told if he were to have any chance of beating the virus, they would have to clear up the blood infection first. He would need a transfusion immediately.

Looking at his chart again, the doctor said there wasn't much chance for that to happen, as he was 0-negative and only the same blood type could provide the blood. Because of the influx recently of accidents, they were out of 0-negative blood. Noah said immediately, "I'm 0 -negative, I can give to him."

"Do you really want to do that…think about it. Giving a transfusion will leave you weak and with all that is going on right now, do you think that's wise?"

Noah stopped for a moment and then replied, "Well, I can save a life right now, and hope it doesn't prevent me from finishing my shift…or I can walk away, knowing I'm signing his death warrant. There's really no question—I'll do it."

Watching his blood flow into the old man's vein, he again wondered what his story was. He had obviously loved someone during his life and he hoped to find out more about it. Maybe there was someone to notify, someone who would sit with him and give him the will to live. If this transfusion worked he might come out of the coma and be communicable again. Time would tell.

Chapter 45

Thinking back to that Thanksgiving dinner so long ago, Noah was again reminded of why he had made infectious disease protocol his major. Arriving at Katie's parents' home, they were greeted with hugs and kisses. Noah was reminded how it felt when Ma and Pa had greeted him the same way. It had been some years since they had passed, but Noah would never forget those wonderful people.

Dinner was delicious and the company was fun and entertaining. He was regaled by stories of Katie's youth and laughed at her embarrassment. The moment came when they were all around the fire, winding down for the evening. Clearing his throat, Noah stood up. As all eyes were on him, he knelt down in front of Katie. As he pulled the little jeweler's box from his pocket, there was an audible gasp from the room.

Katie's hand flew up to her heart and her eyes were brimming with unshed tears. Noah took her hand and looked lovingly into her eyes. "I knew the moment I first laid eyes on you and followed you to your classroom—not a stalker really!—nervous laughter broke out—that I wanted you to be my wife. There's only been a few people in my life that I have loved unconditionally and you are one of them. Would you do me the greatest honor and marry me?"

Katie threw her arms around him and excitedly said yes. When his choice of ring was displayed, there were more tears. It was breathtaking and so heartfelt.

Katie was not only excited about Noah's proposal, but also because the grand opening of her home for needy girls was less than a week away. They had thought long and hard what the name should be, but when Noah gave his suggestion they all knew it was just right. "*Katie's Heart*," he said.

Katie at first resisted not wanting to take credit. "Honey, this whole thing was your idea, your parents are funding it and you will be volunteering there.

It is perfect." Her parents were thrilled with the choice, and when Noah gave that special heart-shaped ring to Katie, everyone was in tears.

As they packed up and got ready to go back to school, there were more tears and rounds of hugs. Again Noah thought how lucky he was and so grateful for God's hand in guiding him through the pain in his past. They set out early Monday morning. It was a beautiful fall day, sunny and crisp. Katie could not stop looking at her ring and smiling at her good fortune. They could not know that their world was about to fall apart.

Chapter 46

The day went quickly and he finally had a moment to check in on Shane. He had slipped into a semi-conscious state and the fever had not broken. His chest was tight and his breathing difficult. There wasn't much more they could do for him, except wait and hope the medication would kick in. Noah tried to get more information from him about his family, but his feverish mumbling was incoherent.

Noah spoke to the admitting nurse when Shane had been admitted and found that she too, was showing symptoms. When he asked her what had been her protocol when she admitted Shane, she told him she had simply washed her hands. Fearing the worst, he sent her for blood tests.

Noah told her to remove herself from duty and place herself in isolation until the tests were back. He called another nurse in to replace her and explained what she must do to protect herself. She must wear a mask and gown, as well as gloves, and they must all be replaced each time they left a room. He then called an emergency meeting with the staff to find out if any other cases of this virus had shown up today.

Two other doctors admitted they'd had similar cases. One had used the usual protocol, while the other doctor had fully gowned himself. The doctor who had not worn a gown or mask was already showing signs of the infection. Although he had not begun to cough, his fever was elevated and his throat was scratchy. Fearing a wide-scale epidemic, Noah called his supervisor and explained what had happened and what his fears were.

Agreeing with him, they made the difficult decision to shut down the hospital. All further patients were to be re-routed to other hospitals in the area and no-one would be allowed in or out until they had this epidemic under control. They began a complex check of patients who were displaying symptoms—and who they had come in contact with.

This was a nightmare trying to find out everyone who they had seen before they arrived in the ER. All staff who had not followed the full protocol were segregated. They would all have to be tested and cleared before they could leave after their shift. The logistics of this were staggering, as space was very limited. Patients and staff displaying symptoms had to be immediately quarantined and the numbers were only increasing.

Space was not Noah's only problem. His supply of antibiotics was dwindling fast and even the basic IV bags and oxygen masks were becoming scarce. Clean laundry was almost nonexistent and they were running out of linens as the cleaning staff were unable to keep up with the demands. Because they had no idea how long the lock down would be, deliveries of food and beverages had been stopped, so as a consequence those were being rationed as well.

The only bit of good news, was that since implementing the full protocol procedures, there had been no new cases reported.

Noah was exhausted and afraid. He was down one doctor and three nurses. The isolated had to be closely monitored—to either clear them or place them in quarantine—and there was still the daunting task of figuring out who was patient 'O', to determine where this had all started.

Noah had to call in more help. After relaying their plight to other hospitals in the area, he was loaned 2 more nurses and 2 doctors. The best news of all was that this was a team trained in full-body containment being sent to help them. He was excited to see an actual trained team at work. They may have newer and more specific ways of dealing with outbreaks such as this.

Even with everything on his shoulders, Noah did not forget about the young boy Shane. He continued to slip in and out of consciousness. His oxygen levels had to be closely monitored and adjusted as needed. His fever had finally broken however, so there was some cause for optimism. During moments of lucidity, Shane was able to tell Noah that his Auntie and Lily had gone to hospital, but that was all he knew. He also stated he had been unable to contact his Dad yet.

He did not know which hospital his Auntie and little sister had gone to. Looking at his chart, the next of kin showed Auntie's name and address. Noah wasn't familiar with that area of New York City, so he had to make enquiries as to which hospitals served that area. He found 2 hospitals that they may have gone to.

He located them at the 2nd hospital. The young girl Lily was symptom free, but the Auntie was showing early signs of infection. Noah explained what they were dealing with and what precautions they must implement to stop the spread of this virulent strain of virus.

It was after 9 o'clock and Noah had not eaten since lunch. Having given blood to the old man, he was starting to feel unsteady and knew he must eat something to keep his strength up.

Afterwards, feeling a bit better he again tried to figure out how to contact Shane's Dad. God only knew how many others he could have infected in his travels. They could never hope to contain this epidemic if they couldn't reach every single person that his Dad had come in contact with…and then everyone they had come in contact with. It seemed to be an impossible task.

Checking in on his old patient, he indeed found him conscious and alert. "They told me you gave me your own blood to make me better," he said. "No-one's ever done anything like that for me before. I've had a hard life, son, and been alone most of the time. How can I ever thank you?"

"There's no need, Sir, it was my pleasure. But there is one thing I'd like to ask you."

"Sure, go ahead."

"Well, when you were semi-conscious you seemed to be saying 'my love, my love'. I thought you said you had no-one in your life."

"Oh son, that was many, many years ago when I was a young man."

"Well, she must have been pretty special for you to remember her for so long."

"She was. She was the love of my life. But I made the damn fool decision to walk away and when I came to my senses and returned to get her, she had left. I had no way of finding her. But I never forgot our sweet romance, not ever."

"How romantic, can you tell me a little more?"

"It was the end of season barn dance and—"

"Wait, what?"

"She was a beauty," the old man smilingly continued, not even hearing Noah's exclamation. "We danced all night and under the stars, we fell in love. When the snow came, I foolishly left to follow the crops. I never saw her again." Stunned, Noah leaned in closer and looked into his rheumy eyes. There was no mistaking that shade of blue.

He couldn't speak—he couldn't even think. Noah excused himself and stepped into the hall. Shaking, he ran his hand through his hair. Dear God, was it possible…had he finally just met his father? After composing himself, he returned to his father's bedside. Sitting down, he gently took hold of his hand. Listening in amazement, Noah explained who he was.

"I have a son…you're my son?" he asked. Nodding yes, Noah continued to give him an abbreviated version of his and his mom's life. There was no need to share the horrors both had suffered. Let him have only good memories. "There wasn't much information on your intake form. What is your name, Dad?"

"Michael, Michael Finlay."

Noah leaned down, and as those two brilliant blue eyes connected (one pair a bit duller with age) he whispered, "Hello Dad, I'm your son." Tears had formed in both their eyes, as his Dad tried to sit up to hug him. Noah carefully helped him up and they gently hugged for what seemed like minutes. It actually was only for a few seconds, as his Dad was very frail.

Looking up at this tall, soft-spoken man, he said, "Your beautiful mother couldn't have raised you any better. Just to know I have a son…" he stopped as he got choked up. "My son is a Doctor," he said in awe. " You are obviously a very smart man, a very kind soul and most importantly, a good man. You gave your blood to who you thought was a complete stranger—Noah, I can't begin to tell her how proud of you I am. You have made whatever time I have left a complete joy. I may not know you well, Son, but I know I love you.

"Your mother would have been so proud of you as well…it couldn't have been easy raising a child on her own…but look at you now." Smiling, he fell back into the bed and began to wheeze.

Noah could see that this all had taken a toll on him and so he said he would see him tomorrow. "Just rest up Dad, you still have to beat this bug."

"My son," he murmured sleepily, "my son." He fell into a deep sleep with a tender smile on his face.

As Noah changed his gown and mask, he went to Shane's room shaking his head. He still could not believe what had just happened. His Mum had told him the love story many times about the soft-spoken man who had swept her away that night under the canopy of twinkling stars. She told him that she would pray always, that one day they would meet. *Well Mum, your prayers have been answered*, Noah thought.

Snapping back to the present, he looked at Shane and said, "Son, can you tell me the name of your Dad's company or the route he always took? It's vital that we locate every person your Dad came in contact with."

Weakened by the virus, Shane replied with some difficulty. "I don't know the exact route, but Dad has a copy of all of his customers at his office."

Just replying to Noah had used up what little strength he had left. "What office, son—what is the company called?" Noah feared Shane could not hear him.

Shane spoke softly, his breathing labored, "Two'fer…it's called Two'fer— we work twice as hard—for half the pay." With that, Shane slipped into unconsciousness again.

Noah looked at Shane in disbelief. It couldn't be—it wasn't possible, he thought. He stumbled back a couple of steps and stood staring at the young boy. Several seconds went by until Noah realized his mouth was hanging open. Quickly closing his mouth before someone noticed the state he was in, he grabbed a local phone book and flipped to the yellow pages and searched for seafood suppliers. His hand was shaking as he scrolled down the short list.

There, under the 'T's was a company named 'Two'fer'…its logo read: 'We work twice as hard—for half the pay'.

Underneath the picture of a large red lobster was the owner's name…'Kaleb Enterprises'.

Chapter 47

He was almost through half of his deliveries, but his usual pace had slowed significantly, as he had been feeling pretty rough all morning. His throat was really scratchy and he'd started to cough. Spring colds were the worst he thought. They seemed to last forever. Heading back to his hotel room for a quick bite and a bit of a rest before finishing up for the day, he began coughing in earnest.

Tears sprang to his eyes from the exertion and the extended hacking left him very weak. He decided to try his sister again. There had been no answer at her house all morning and he was beginning to get worried. Where was she and his 7-year-old daughter, Lily? Again reaching no-one, he slammed the phone down in anger and frustration. What was going on?

He had been unable to contact his son Shane either. Something was wrong—he could feel it.

Unable to finish lunch—he sat back and debated what to do. He knew a few of Shane's friends, but they must all be at their jobs now. Searching his memory, he recalled where two of his buddies worked. The last one he called was able to help him. He told Kaleb that Shane had felt really bad the last few days, and was finally convinced to go in and get checked out. The friend went on to say he hadn't seen Shane since.

There were 3 hospitals in that part of the city, so Kaleb began calling them one-by-one and was rewarded on his second try. "Yes sir, we do have a patient admitted under that name, but unless you are a family member, we are not able to give out any information for privacy reasons, you understand."

"Well, I am his father and am out of town for a few more days. I am also not getting any answer from my sister whose is looking after my 7-year-old daughter." Raising his voice, Kaleb stated, "You either tell me what's wrong with my son, or give me someone who can. NOW!"

The young nurse, frightened from his tone, put him on hold and rushed to get a Doctor. Since Noah had gone home for the evening, another doctor filled Kaleb in on his son's condition. "His chart shows he is responding to the medication, but he must remain in hospital until we are sure he is fully recovered. It also shows that his Aunt and little sister were assessed at Mercy Hospital and the child was symptom-free."

Thank God, Kaleb thought.

"Your sister, however, was showing early onset symptoms and was placed in quarantine as a precaution. If the tests come back negative, she will be free to go. If not, we will start her on the recommended medication and watch her closely for any improvement."

"But what has become of my daughter Lily?" Kaleb asked with a touch of hysteria in his voice.

"Don't worry Sir, she was picked up by her other Aunt who, after being cleared, brought her home. They are both fine. However, I must insist you present yourself immediately to the nearest hospital to be checked out. Also, please make a list of everyone you have come in contact with during the last 3 days. Please have the hospital forward a copy to us. This is vital if we are to contain this outbreak."

"Very well, I'll go right now," Kaleb assured the doctor. After being tested, he was relieved to hear he did not have the virus and that it was just a severe cold.

Chapter 48

Arriving home again, Noah was in a daze. The last of his shift had been a blur. First he found his father who he never thought he'd ever meet, and then to find out Kaleb was here—in New York City? How was that possible? How long had it been? Thinking back to that earlier time, he had been only 16 years old. He had just turned 39—that meant 23 years had passed since they had last seen each other. That would make Kaleb 42! Opening a can of something for dinner (he didn't even know what it was), Noah sank into his chair, his thoughts swirling in his head.

Finally feeling exhausted, he fell into a much needed sleep. Even the extraordinary circumstances of today could not keep him awake. He dreamt of the many years he had prayed for a real dad, how he longed for that connection. He remembered the old man in the hospital room and how, somehow he seemed to be intrigued by his story—or lack thereof. His decision to give him his own blood was even for him, extraordinary. But he had definitely felt a compulsion to do so. And then to find out that he was his father?

He now had a true last name, he dreamt happily. Finlay…He was Noah Finlay. Smiling at the marvels of the Universe and how God answers prayers on His schedule, Noah finally fell into a deep sleep.

Getting up the next day, Noah was anxious to get to the hospital. He wanted to get there a bit early, so he could check on his dad and spent a little time with him before his shift started. As he walked down the hallway, his thoughts travelled back in time, to a small coastal area where most families relied on farming and fishing to survive.

He remembered the little farming area where he first met Kaleb. He remembered the hardships their families suffered. Back then, the economy being what it was, a boy had only two options for his future—farming what little land they had, or becoming a fisherman in one of the little coastal villages. There was no expectations of higher learning—'book smarts' was not encouraged. The goal of young men was simply to start helping their families as quickly as possible through manual labor.

Memories came flooding back, of a young Kaleb and even younger Noah setting off to find greener pastures. Oh, at first it was exciting—seeing and doing things they'd never done before. But always in the backs of their young minds, they remembered the desperate circumstances their families faced. They were determined to make things better for their loved ones. Their shared hardships and common goals created a tight bond between them—they were brothers for life!.

But the best of plans, even with the truest intentions can go astray. Noah stayed behind to study medicine, while Kaleb followed the fishing. On that fateful last day together, they both pledged that they would keep in touch, but apart from a couple of more visits, and the exchange of a few letters (yes, he had learned to write!), even that had stopped.

Since then, Noah had heard absolutely nothing from this man, who had been his best friend, his mentor, his partner in all of their dreams of the future—his 'big brother'. This man who shared so many painful memories of their childhood, who got Noah through so many ups and downs, was now in New York after 23 years! It was truly amazing.

Noah had just pushed through the doors when a fellow doctor spotted him. "Hey pal, have some bad news for you. That old man that you gave a transfusion to yesterday passed away through the night. Tough luck, sorry, man."

Noah stopped dead in his tracks. Dead? He wasn't that bad when he left him last night. How did this happen? He went looking for his chart. The room was empty and the cleaning staff were already cleaning it for the next patient. Still in shock he went to patients records. Trying to stay calm, he asked the clerk if he could see the records for the recently passed Michael Finlay. Opening the file up, he quickly scanned the information.

It showed that his dad had relapsed and needed oxygen once more. By early morning, his oxygen had maxed out. There was nothing else they could do. His father's death was at 4:44 a.m.

Sitting down, Noah put his head in his hands and cried. Why would God bring his father into his life—only to take him away the next day? He sat there shattered. Because Noah had not shared his reunion with his Dad, the hospital staff had no idea that the old man was his father. They certainly would not have been so cavalier with the information had they known.

Noah was inconsolable. All he could think of was the many years he had been cheated out of precious time with his Dad. How like his Mum, he had secretly always wished to one day come face-to-face with the man that had swept his Mum off her feet so many years ago. He had come to believe finally after all these years, it just wasn't meant to be.

Slowly, his thought process cleared. Instead of raging at God for this cruel twist of fate, Noah realized that it was a blessing he had been given, to actually meet his dad before he left this world. He smiled sadly as he remembered the look of joy on his dad's face when he looked at his only child. His anger with God changed to feelings of gratitude. That he was able to see those blue eyes—his eyes—so filled with pride was truly a gift.

Gathering his wits about him, Noah knew what he had to do. After arranging with the morgue to transfer his dad's body to a nearby crematorium, he was able to have some closure. If he hadn't met this man, his dad would have died alone and been buried in the potter's field. Now, he would bring him home and give him the respect he deserved. This settled, Noah went on with his day.

Going forward, Noah remembered Shane and Kaleb. Noah subconsciously shook his head, as so many emotions filled his mind. Shock, happiness, elation, excitement, confusion; and truth be told, even a little uneasiness was present. What, after all this time, would a reunion be like? Would he be happy to see him? Would they immediately fall back into their old, comfortable banter? Or would it be strained and awkward between them?

Noah had the upper hand, he thought, in this unfolding drama. He knew that Kaleb had been married, had 2 children, and at least 2 of his sisters lived right here in New York City. Records showed his wife had succumbed to cancer several years ago. Kaleb would be stunned to find out that Noah had become a doctor…and that he was actually treating his son!

What would this reunion be like? he thought. Would it be like old times…picking up as if no time had passed? Or would it be awkward and uncomfortable…Time would tell…

Chapter 49

As they entered the tunnel, the lights of an oncoming car blinded them. Brakes squealing, the two vehicles hit with such force that their car turned over two times, swerving into yet another vehicle, finally coming to rest in the middle of the tunnel. Noah remembered Katie screaming in fear and then everything went black…

Something was wrong…he couldn't move. Everything was fuzzy and his eyes could not focus. Noah tried to reach out in the semi-darkness but was trapped in place by his seatbelt. His heart was beating furiously as he tried to calm himself. Blackness crept into his peripheral vision as he again lost consciousness…

Chapter 50

Several days passed and no new cases of the virus had surfaced. "Well done, Noah, you've proven your protocols really work. They will now become standard practices at this, and many more hospitals. Congratulations! Cheers and a round of applause broke out among the nurses and doctors gathered.

"Speech, speech," they chanted good-heartedly.

Noah, smiling embarrassed, faced the crowd. "Thank you—thank you all, but this was a group effort. We never would have been able to contain this virus without everyone on board." At this point, spontaneous applause broke out again. Putting up his hand, Noah continued, "It was the dedicated team work. your selflessness and hard work that turned the tide. I am truly blessed to work with what I believe is the best trauma team in New York City. Thank you all very much."

Backing away from the cheering crowd, Noah gave one last smile and exited the cafeteria. He'd managed to hide his distress of talking to the crowd very well, but he was glad that was over.

Now he could get back to work.

Horns beeping, people screaming, the smell of gasoline. Horrified, Noah looked around frantically for Katie. It was almost impossible to see in the dark tunnel with the smoke and flames increasing. She wasn't in the car...where could she be? Noah suddenly remembered the moments before the crash. Katie had just unbuckled her seatbelt to lean over to give him a kiss...*Oh my God*, he thought, *where is she?*

Things began to fade out as he succumbed to the encroaching blackness once again. He woke once more to the sound of emergency vehicles and the shrill sound of metal grinding. They were extricating him, but all he could think of was Katie. Again he found himself sinking into oblivion. When next he awoke, he was travelling in an ambulance. He repeatedly asked about Katie

144

but was told it had been a multi-car accident with several ambulances having been called. They would know more when they arrived at the hospital.

Entering Shane's room, he saw Kaleb sitting by his bed. As Kaleb met Noah's eyes…something clicked. His eyes widened and he jumped up from his chair. "Noah…is it really you?" he exclaimed.

Noah laughed and embraced his old friend. "You know Doc Noah, Dad?" Shane asked.

Noah answered, "Your father and I go way back, Shane…way way back. We were best friends and shared a great adventure one summer 23 years ago," Noah said smiling.

"No kidding? Dad, you never told me any of this?"

"Well son, it never seemed to be the right time…but I guess there's no time like the present." As the two men embraced again, it seemed like the years had all slipped away and they were, once again, best buddies. Kaleb invited Noah for dinner and said he would cook him the best lobster he'd ever eaten. They arranged a time and agreed that they couldn't wait to catch up on each other's lives since parting so long ago. Shane was doubly excited as he knew he was in for one heck of an adventure!

Chapter 51

The meal was excellent. The lobster was sweet and succulent and the wine was perfect. As they ate, there was a lot of laughing and good-natured ribbing. "Yes well, you should have seen Noah's first day on the boat—he spent most of it hanging over the side spilling his guts out." Kaleb laughed. Shane thought that was too funny and laughed so hard he almost choked on a piece of fish.

Noah continued, "Oh really? I seem to recall the day your Dad was shoveling salt into the hole, slipped, and fell head first into all the fish! I think someone suggested throwing that big flopping one back into the ocean!"

Again Shane laughed. "Wow, you guys seemed to have the best summer ever," he said wistfully.

"Well lad, it wasn't all fun and games. We had to leave our homes and families to try and find work to support them. To leave all you knew and loved behind for an uncertain future was very, very hard. You have no way to know how life is going to throw you a curve ball so big that you think you'll never be able to handle it. But you do, and I guess that's part of becoming a man," Noah said thoughtfully.

"Yes son, sometimes growing up can be pretty painful—some lessons are hard to take, but as Noah says…we deal with whatever God gives us and hopefully become better for it."

"It builds character, Pa always said," Noah smiled.

"Was that your Dad, Noah?" Shane asked. Both Noah and Kaleb chuckled at that, as they explained about these two extraordinary people.

"I honestly do not know where I'd be today if these amazingly loving people had not come into my life," Noah confessed.

"Nor I," Kaleb said, "they changed my live forever as well."

After they cleared the dishes, they went into the living room and Kaleb started a fire in the hearth. As he filled his pipe, he asked Noah if he minded if

146

he smoked. "Not at all...did you get that habit from Pa's constitutional?" Noah laughed.

"Yes, as a matter of fact, I did—he left me this pipe. treasure it each time I use it." They settled down on the couch, in front of the roaring fire with Shane at their feet not wanting to miss anything. Both men were anxious to explain the last 23 years of their lives.

Chapter 52

Amid all the chaos, Noah was finally told what happened to Katie. At the point of impact, because she was not wearing her seatbelt, her body was thrown through the windshield. Katie landed 30 feet away and was severely burned. She suffered deep lacerations to her upper body and face and was in critical condition.

Noah's heart broke. He had come out relatively unscathed with only a broken collarbone, minor cuts and contusions, and a slight concussion. After patching him up. they brought him to Katie's room to wait for her return from surgery. They had called in a facial reconstruction surgeon and had a burn unit waiting for her.

Several hours later, they told Noah that she had come out of surgery and was downgraded to serious. Noah was allowed to see her for only a few minutes. Her face was unrecognizable and her upper torso was swathed in bandages. They had her on a morphine drip to reduce the pain. She was thankfully unconscious for the first couple of days. As she began to come out of the coma, the pain was unbearable. Noah insisted they up her morphine levels to give her more respite.

Every day Noah would sit by her bedside. As she began the slow process of healing, the doctors were hopeful that she would recover. She would never look the same, they explained but she would be able to have a life. Her face was healing fairly well, but the deep tissue burns were another matter. It was torture to have to watch her endure the constant changing of the dressings.

She screamed throughout the whole procedure, as removing the dirty bandages always peeled back several layers of skin. through all of the agony that she suffered, Noah never left her alone. Finally, after several weeks her face'had healed and the bandages removed.

She was loathe to look in a mirror, but Noah told her over and over he loved her no matter what. As Katie continued to improve slightly and be able to talk again (although too much was painful), she had only one thing on her mind. What was happening with *Katie's Heart*?

Noah quickly assured her that they had gone ahead as planned with the opening and that five lucky young girls had been given a second chance at life. Relief crossed Katie's face as she slumped back in bed. "One of your fellow students, Shelly Capshaw had volunteered to fill until you were better and could return," Noah continued.

"Shelly, she's a sweetheart, she'll be a great fit," Katie said contentedly. Her parents were devastated and were constant visitors as well. They kept her up-to-date with the running of the girl's home and told her that all the girls there were praying for her swift recovery. They wanted Katie to know how much it meant to them that someone would love and want to care for them as Katie did.

The girls had all written heart-filled letters to Katie to show their love and gratitude. This brought Katie much happiness. She would read and re-read those letters daily. They always seemed to give her the strength to carry on.

The only thing keeping her in hospital now, was the devastating burns. At first Noah was not aware of the lack of preventative hygiene when dealing with Katie. He just had too many other things to deal with. But gradually, he noticed that no precautions were being taken when entering her room. Even as a lowly post grad student, Noah felt they were not practicing safe protocol.

That last day they changed her bandages, he knew something was wrong. It brought him right back to the day his leg had gotten infected on the boat. Horrified, he watched as they removed a length of bandage that was green and putrefied. It was obvious that it was infected. They immediately started her on intravenous antibiotics, but it was too little, too late. The infection had been too deep for the antibiotics to overcome.

Noah and Katie's parents held a vigil with her, as they held her hands and sang softly to her. No-one would leave her side. But to no avail. The love of his life slipped into a coma and succumbed a few days later. At first, Noah was too shattered to realize the implications of poor hygiene, but as time went on, it was obvious what had killed Katie. It wasn't the accident…it wasn't the surgeries…it wasn't the initial trauma to her body. It was simply no preventive disease precautions. Had there been a plan in place where strict hygiene protocol was implemented, Katie would still be alive today.

Noah decided then and there to devote his time and energies to try and prevent such needless deaths from ever happening again.

Chapter 53

"After we left you there in the hospital, the mood was pretty somber on the boat. Pa was quiet and Ma went about her duties except she kept dabbing at her eyes every few minutes. Supper that night wasn't Ma's usual grand affair, as she just didn't seem to care much about what she was preparing. Everyone was subdued—there would be no singing that evening.

"It was a long night and I have to admit I was pretty lonely looking over at your empty bunk. But the next day…things were pretty much back to normal…Pa saw to that. At the breakfast table, Pa said we all missed you but that if we wanted to eat this winter we had to get back to work.

"He said, 'All hands on deck…I want a full day's work from everyone.' He probably knew the best thing for everyone was to keep busy. Anyway, after we got through that first day, all the others didn't seem so bad. The nets were full, the weather stayed clear and the strong winds helped us stay on track. We only had a couple of weeks left in the season and we were in good spirits.

"On our last return to your 'adopted' village, we all were excited to see you. Ma couldn't contain herself…she even baked cookies just for you. Do you remember them? No-one else was allowed to touch them…you fancied yourself pretty special when she told you that." Kaleb laughed.

"Oh my God…I do remember them! They were so good." Noah laughed.

"Our visit was too short though as we had to leave the next morning. It was so hard leaving you again, but it was obvious to everyone that you were thriving there and you had found your calling. Before they left, Ma and Pa handed you a small envelope. 'Here's your pay for your work on board,' Pa said gruffly. 'I can't take this,' you said but Pa insisted, saying no-one worked for free on his boat.

"The trip back was obviously very hard on Ma the most, as no-one knew when we would actually see you again. I know her big heart was breaking but she tried really hard not to show it. When we returned home, Ma made me a special going-away dinner. I was leaving to go home to take care of my Ma and brother and sisters. I had made enough money to get us through the winter.

"Not wanting to leave these precious people, I asked if I could return next spring and fish with them again. Ma cried, saying she had been praying I would want to. She and Pa said I was welcomed back every year. During the return trip home, I had no trouble with the dogs or the mountain." He laughed.

"You should have seen my Mum's face when I showed up at the door. She was glowing. The joy just radiated off her. She held my little brother up to me, but he didn't seem so little anymore! The twins came tumbling into my arms but the older girls seemed shy at first until I picked them up and swung them around. They collapsed in giggles. It was a good day.

"I walked up to Ma and hugged her so tight I thought I might hurt her. Tears were streaming down her face, for me, for your Ma and for you. I explained all that had happened that summer and told her all about the wonderful couple who had taken us into their home and into their hearts. I told her that I was welcomed to come back every fishing season, and Ma looked peaceful for the first time I can remember. She said that God had answered her prayers more than once this year and that we were blessed.

"So I worked around the farm fixing things that needed fixing and helped Ma get the vegetables ready for the winter. I kept in touch with Ma and Pa and they said they had gotten a letter from you. Just a short note really but they were impressed! You had explained that one of the older nurses had made you her 'special' project and that her Christmas gift to you was to teach you to read and write. I remember I wrote you a note that simply said 'Prove it, love, Kaleb!'

"Laughing, you wrote back 'Told you so, love, Noah!' I laughed for days. Ma thought it was great—you learning and all. By spring, I was ready to go fishing again. I missed the boat, the other mates, the open sea, and most of all, I missed Ma and Pa who seemed like a Granny and Grandpa to me."

Chapter 54

"Kissing Ma and the kids goodbye, I started off for my second fishing season. This time though, I was confident and unafraid. I knew what lay ahead and was anxious to begin. During that season, we all got to see you again. We were all shocked at how you had grown. It was another good year and I went home again and did pretty much what I had the year before.

"The last time we saw each other was the next year when I was 19 and you had just turned 16. This last meeting was different than the others. It seemed we had both changed, grown up—maybe even grown apart? Anyway, it was very cordial but something was missing. I think I realized that we had both grown and were on different paths. It was bittersweet. I remember we hugged for the last time and said we'd keep in touch…but of course, we didn't. Time and distance had taken its toll."

Noah shook his head in sad agreement. "I thought we would be together forever…that I would grow old with my 'big brother'. I'm sure God looks down on us making all our plans…making all our lists and chuckles at the audacity that we actually think we are in control of our destiny. Yes, that first time you left me was heartbreaking to me too, as I not only was losing my best friend and my big brother but I was an orphan now and was now losing Ma and Pa, the only family I had left."

"Well Noah, there was another reason we didn't get to see you after that last time," Kaleb continued. "The lanes we had been fishing in were depleted and Pa said we would have to change our course and go further out if we were to be able to eat that winter. Ma took it very hard—not being able to see you. We all knew you had been her favorite—something about you just touched her heart. She never seemed quite the same after that.

"There was a sadness about her—an empty space I think in her heart. Pa seemed to have more quiet spells himself, just looking off into space. It was hard to see some of the life go out of these two wonderful people. They were clearly pining away for you. But the fishing was good in these new lanes and time passed quickly.

"Several seasons in, Ma took sick. Pa was beside himself. As my siblings were mostly all grown, my Mum agreed to let me stay the winter with Ma and Pa to help out. I sent money home as always and settled in to help these kind souls who had become my family.

"How I loved them, Noah. It seemed the more Ma deteriorated—Pa would follow suit. It was heartbreaking to watch them both fail like that…it seemed that Pa had just given up and was determined to leave this world with his beloved Ma. By early spring…they were both gone. They died through the night, holding hands.

"When they were laid to rest, a man came to speak to me. He was short and portly and said he had been their lawyer and had known them most of their lives. They had told him all about you and I and said we were the kids they never had. They said they had heard you were studying to become a doctor and were so proud of you.

"Knowing how expensive schooling would be, they wanted to leave you their savings to help with that. Knowing you would do well for yourself, they wanted to ensure I would have a good future as well. They left me their treasured boat and little house. Of course, I was already aware of their wishes as they had talked to me at length about them.

"I decided to keep their house for it was filled with so many loving memories. I became Captain of the boat and continue the yearly fishing. Each year after sending money back to my Mum, I was able to put aside a tidy sum, as I lived quite simply.

"Within a few years, I was able to buy a second boat. I too did some studying, Noah…to find out where the best market would be for selling my fish. That's how I came to New York City where I fell in love.

"I had an appointment at the bank to discuss opening up my business. The loans manager was smart as a whip and also the most gorgeous girl I had ever seen. Even after Gracie approved my loan, I kept inventing reasons to go into the bank. Finally, she laughingly said, 'We have to stop meeting like this.' I was smitten. We started dating and Gracie was pivotal in starting up my business. She had it all—brains and beauty and I remember asking her how I got so lucky.

"We worked together and planned out our whole lives. The day we found out she was having our first baby was one of the most happiest days of my life. When Shane was born, our lives were complete. Each year was better than the last. Our home was filled with love and laughter. When we found out she was pregnant again, we were ecstatic. But our happy days were numbered.

"Shortly after we found out we were expecting again, Gracie started to get tired more easily. She brushed it off at first, thinking our lives were just too busy. But her lack of energy wouldn't go away. Finally, I convinced her to see a doctor. The news was devastating. She had stage four breast cancer.

"The doctors advised her to begin treatment right away, but she refused. She would not put our child at risk. I tried to tell her we could have other children…to just get healthy first, but she refused to even consider it. Each day, I watched her get weaker and weaker."

Chapter 55

"She decided she would make memory books for Shane and the little one on the way. She knew her time was limited and she wanted to leave something for them to remember her by. She spent hours cutting up pictures, writing little notes and decorating the two scrapbooks. They were beautiful, each one individualized for her children. Shane's was filled with a multitude of pictures and loving remembrances."

"I still have mine, Dad, and I will always treasure it," Shane said softly through eyes brimming with unshed tears.

"I know son, that's why Mom made it for you. She loved you and Lily so much. It was her way of staying close to you.

"Lily's had all of her sonogram pictures in it along with the dates of every doctor's appointment. We took pictures of her drawing in Lily's book, of her holding what would be her first teddy bear and everything else we could think of. She wrote little notes to be read on each of her birthdays and a special letter for her wedding day.

"Each night we hugged in bed, whispering sweet nothings to each other, as if it were our last night together. I truly believe her illness brought us closer together in some strange way. I spent all my time with her and Shane, storing memories that would have to last a lifetime. Not everything was memorable though, as I watched her go through many painful moments. There was the day when I walked in to finding Gracie huddled in a heap on the floor, sobbing uncontrollably.

"Rushing to her, I knelt down and asked what was wrong. She looked up through her tears and replied, 'I've smashed Shane's picture...the one he made me for Mother's Day.' Her body was shaking and she was full of anguish. 'But honey, it's just the frame that's broken—look—his picture is fine. We'll get another frame, that's all.'

"Falling into my arms, she finally calmed down. As I helped her up to bed, she looked at me and said, 'How would I ever get through this without you?' 'You will never have to my love, I will always be with you.'

"Then there was the day I found her on the bathroom floor weeping and mortified that she had not made it to the toilet in time. Lovingly, I cleaned her up and laid down with her in bed. I stroked her hair until she fell asleep. I watched as my beautiful, vibrant wife became frail and wracked with pain.

"Those were tough days for sure. Hard times can break a couple apart if the love is not there. But with us, if brought us closer, to be able to share the good and the bad times together. True love means true commitment and we were blessed to have that."

Chapter 56

"The day Lily was born was a miracle. Although she was weak, Gracie's face was glowing. Just looking into that sweet little face made everything worthwhile. Bringing Lily home was a blessing. Shane fell in love the moment he looked into Lily's eyes. I knew he would be the best big brother ever."

Shane smiled sadly.

"Although she was very weak, Grace insisted we eat dinner each night together. She made it special with candles and the 'fancy' plates. She said, 'No more waiting for special occasions—every day is a special occasion for us now.' She did not have the strength to cook big meals anymore—so apart from the occasional take-out, I became chief cook and bottle washer!

"But even a pizza delivered got the 5-star treatment...candles and all! I actually became quite comfortable in the kitchen...what do you say about that, Shane?" he chuckled.

"Yes Dad, you weren't bad—not as good as Mom, but not bad."

"Each milestone in Lily's first year was of colossal importance. More pictures, more loving notes. She lived to see Lily's first birthday. I remember it like it was just yesterday. She awoke that morning weaker than ever, as the night had been rough. The pain had robbed her of much needed rest and she looked pale. She refused to give into the increasing pain however, as she was determined not to miss Lily's first birthday. She probably knew that this would be her last birthday shared with Lily.

"She asked me to help her get up and ready for the festivities. Although she was unable to partake physically, I carried her downstairs and placed her gently on the wing chair by the fire. She was so thin, it was like carrying a small child," Kaleb remembered. "After tucking a cozy blanket around her...the party came to her. Gracie's eyes glowed with happiness as she watched Shane and I blow up the balloons...well, really just me...Shane wasn't much help."

"Hey!" Shane laughed.

Chuckling, Kaleb continued, "Well, Shane did help me string up the birthday banner. It was not just any banner, it was a special banner we put up every year. Each year it is signed and I'm not sure what we'll do when we run out of space! The presents were placed at Gracie's feet in preparation of the big opening after supper.

"As we settled around the table prepared to eat Lily's favorite meal (kraft dinner and chicken nuggets—yum), Gracie began with a special grace, 'I want to say how grateful to our Heavenly Father I am, for all the love and joy He has brought into our lives.'

"As she continued softly, her face seemed to glow in the candlelight. 'Some people might think I have no reason to be grateful to God because of what I'm going through…but they would be wrong. I'm especially grateful because of what I'm going through. Pain and sadness only highlights the happy times and we are so much more aware and appreciate those happy times because of it. Our joy is only increased because we remember the sad times. My message to you, my dear ones, is to always remember the good and the bad…but to focus on the good. It will get you through the bad in the future. Live through the bad times—and live for the good times. Remember how much I love you all and I will always be with you, just a thought away.'

"Lily seemed to agree, as just as Gracie fell silent, Lily started to giggle. Her innocent laughter broke up the hush that had descended over the table.

"After a filling meal of haute cuisine…(although Gracie was unable to eat much), we retired to the living room. Placing Lily at her feet amongst the many presents, Gracie laughingly watched as Lily tore into the pile. I could tell the pain was escalating by Gracie's grimaces, but she was determined to stay up till the end.

"My oldest sister had helped us out for some time now with the bathing and getting the kids to bed, so after she took Lily upstairs Gracie allowed me to bring her up to bed. She insisted on reading Shane a story, while hugging him close. When it was time for Shane to go to bed, Gracie hugged him fiercely, not wanting him to go. As my eyes misted over, I picked him up and put Shane to bed. We both knew that this was Gracie's final farewell to her beloved son."

"I'd never heard that before, Dad, it makes me so sad."

"No son, remember what Mom said about letting go of the sadness and remembering the good times?"

"Yes—but sometimes it's not easy."

"I know, Shane, but anything worthwhile is never easy.

"When I returned to Gracie, I saw she had sunk further down in the pillows. She whispered for me to bring in Lily. I placed Lily between us and took Gracie's hand. It was so small, childlike. Her grip was strong though and as my tears began to fall, Gracie began to sing their favorite song: 'You are my sunshine'. I had heard that song so many times before, but never so tenderly.

"She gazed into my eyes and her love for me filled my soul. I kissed her hand softly as my tears fell freely. Slowly, I felt Gracie's hand loosen in mine and then open...unmoving. With a strangled sob, I picked up Lily who had been sleeping in her mother's arms and took her to her crib. After calling her doctor, I returned to Gracie and held her until the doctor arrived.

"Although my life was shattered, never to be the same again, I was so grateful that she lived to see our business thrive and know our children would never want for anything." Kaleb continued, "And my business is really a family affair, as my brother now drives for me and my two oldest sisters work in the office. The twins though, wanted no part of the fish business," he chuckled, "guess they'd had enough growing up with it. They've chosen a totally different path, but that's another story for another time."

Chapter 57

Laughing, they struggled up the long flight of stairs to their apartment. This was the first time they had ever been on their own. All their lives they had shared a dream…to be writers. While the oldest (by 2 minutes) wanted to write the next great American novel, the younger had dreams of writing screen plays and seeing her work on the big screen.

All their lives, people had trouble telling them apart and they used that to their advantage. While their families could spot the differences right away…teachers and even a boyfriend once were fooled, if only for a little while. They had toyed with the idea of changing their hair or dressing totally different, but they always came back to the same thought.

This was what made them unique…how they had always lived…maybe later as they grew older, had separate lives, but for now they loved their special bond. They had just graduated from college and were looking for work. They knew they'd have to ' pay their dues ' before landing the job of their dreams and were willing to do whatever it took.

Janet and Janey, the JJ twins, were quite a handful. Janey, the youngest (by 2 minutes) had already lined up a job in a bodega just down the street. Janet was still looking. Even a studio apartment cost an arm and a leg in New York City, so money was tight. Trying to find their own space to write in such cramped conditions wouldn't be easy, but they'd make it work. Their older brother offered to help, as his fishing distribution company was doing very well, but they were adamant they would do it on their own.

Her first shift at the bodega was tonight and Janey was excited (and a bit nervous). They had heard all the scary stories about the 'Big Apple' and so they were both a little anxious. But they put that all out of their minds, as young kids do, thinking they're invincible…As Janey was leaving, her sister gave her a big hug and told her to stay safe.

"Don't worry, big sis, I'll be fine." Making herself a cup of tea, Janet went back to searching the paper for jobs. The first shift over, Janey returned to their apartment just after midnight. Janet had stayed up to hear all about the night. "It was great...actually a bit boring...but boring is good, right?" Janey laughed.

"There were only a few customers so I had time to stock the shelves. There was a bit of excitement though, as a police cruiser pulled in around 11 pm lights flashing and everything."

"Oh my God, what happened?" Janet said sitting up straighter in bed.

"They were looking for a couple of kids involved in a shooting, but I told them no-one had come in."

"Wow, you must have been scared."

"Yea I guess, but it sure would make a good screenplay."

Giggling, Janet replied, "As mom always said, if life gives you lemons—make lemonade."

The next day the girls decided to take a walk around their new neighborhood. The sights and sounds were infectious and they laughed and strolled arm and arm. Mouth-watering aromas wafted out of the many little cafes...Greek souvlaki...Mexican tortillas...Italian home cooking...Ukrainian perogies...the selection was never-ending. They could see people doing a double take and one kid on a bike actually drove into a flower cart. They were used to such attention and just giggled even more. They stopped at a cafe to grab a bite to eat. As they were sitting there a young man came up to them. He was smartly dressed and well groomed.

Handing them his card, he introduced himself. He was with a large advertising firm and asked if they'd ever considered a job in commercials. Amused, they said no, that they had no experience with that kind of thing. As he was leaving, he told them to consider it. It would be good money, easy work and could lead to greater things. They thanked him and watched him leave.

"Yea, sure," Janet said, "I'll make you a star—probably want us to do a "Twofer" in some X-rated movie!"

"Oh gross," Janey groaned. They of course knew all about their big brother's childhood and where he had gotten the name for his company. "Once is enough." They both laughed as Janet slipped the card into her pocket.

Each day they adjusted to their little apartment easier. Well, you couldn't really call it an apartment. It was just one big room with a small bath attached.

But necessity is the mother of invention, so they had set up their space well. They found a really pretty pull-out couch (which of course would double as their bed) and placed it under their large picture window.

That window was the nicest thing about the whole room, and when they sat on it in the evening, they could look out at a vista of colored lights and flashing neon. It was beautiful. On the other side of the room was a little galley kitchen that could only fit one at a time, but that was OK as Janey wasn't a cook. She wasn't much of a housekeeper either, her sister joked, so it was just as well they had a small apartment.

Laughing, Janey said, "Well, when my stellar career as a screenwriter takes off, I will have a maid and a cook."

Janey had been working for about a week now at the bodega and had made a few friends. The regular customers really seemed to take to her and apart from the almost continual screaming of police cars and ambulances, things were pretty quiet. It was just after 10 p.m. that night when the jingle of bells announced another customer.

Janey looked up and she caught her breath. A man came running in carrying a gun. He looked to be about 30 years old and was obviously on something. His eyes were wild looking and his wasted body was shaking. Janey immediately thought of the old man at the back of the store. He had come in for milk and she prayed he would stay back there quietly.

Chapter 58

As the druggie came towards the counter, Janey pushed the silent alarm for the police. They would be here in a matter of minutes if she could just get through this. "Gimme the money...all of it NOW," he shouted, pointing the gun at Janey. It looked like an automatic weapon, and Janey's blood ran cold. Fumbling with the cash drawer, he shouted again, "Hurry up or I'll blow your head off."

Janey managed to get the drawer open, pleading with him not to shoot. As she pushed the cash over the counter to him, the wails of the police car startled him. It also startled the old man at the back of the store and he dropped his milk. The bottle smashed on the floor and the thief looked up.

Running to the aisle, he sprayed the back with bullets. The old man fell over dead. Screaming, Janey dropped to her knees behind the counter. As the police ran up to the door, the thief yelled out, "Get back, I just killed an old man and I have a hostage. I want a car and $100,000 or the girl will die." He yanked up Janey, who was sobbing uncontrollably, to prove what he had threatened.

Outside, it was pandemonium. A second police car had arrived along with an ambulance. A crisis team was on the way with a negotiator. The beat cop was speaking into a bull horn. "We hear you and we are working to get the money. As a show of good faith, can you send out the old man?"

"What for—he ain't go nowhere—he's dead." The cop rubbed his head and thought this was above his pay grade. They would have to wait for the negotiator.

Inside, the thief shook Janey and threatened to shoot her too if she didn't stop crying. Slowly, she managed to get herself under control. She thought of Janet and all of their big plans, and she started to cry again, this time softly. "I told you to stop that whining. I already killed tonight...nothing more to lose" he said roughly.

Janey swallowed hard and dried her tears. *Just pretend this is a script I'm writing*, she thought to herself. *Pretend it's a movie.*

Outside, the crisis team had arrived with the negotiator. He grabbed the bullhorn and said calmly, "Hello, my name is Manuel and I am your negotiator. It's my job to get you what you want so we can all go home safely. What is your name?"

"None of your damn business. And why did they send a damn wetback...I want an American."

"Sir, I am an American, my parents were born here and so was I."

"Why the hell they give you that damn spic name then?" Manuel turned and looked at the people around him, shaking his head. Bad enough they were dealing with a drugged-up, murdering thief...but he was a racist too? Some days he asked himself why he had chosen this line of work. He, not for the first time, wondered if he should have become a priest as his mother had always wanted. He would have still been helping people, out of the line of fire (usually) and the retirement package was unrivalled. Shaking his head, he turned back to the scene unfolding before him.

As the news trucks arrived, dozens of reporters flooded the scene. Back at their little apartment, Janet noticed all the flashing lights and police cars at the end of the block. *Wow*, she thought, *something big is going down*. Turning on the TV, she wondered if it was on the news. "And now we are cutting back live to the unfolding scene outside a little bodega on the East side. Reports say that there has already been one killed and a hostage taken. There is a negotiator on-site and we'll have further updates at 11. This is MTG Channel 7 signing off for now."

Janet thought she might pass out. *That has to be where Janey works.* Grabbing her phone, she frantically called her sister's number. No response. Grabbing her coat, she ran out the door. God help us, let Janey be alright. As she came up to the crowd in front of the bodega, she had to push herself through the throng of emergency crews and looky-loos.

She had almost made it to the front when someone grabbed her from behind. "I'm sorry, miss. this is a police matter and an active crime scene. You can't go any further."

"You don't understand officer, my sister works in there, I have to know if she's alright." The officer immediately brought her over to the hostage negotiator. Explaining who she was, he left her. Manuel shook her hand and told her that her sister was alright for now and they were doing their best to keep it that way. Wringing her hands and crying, someone put a cup of coffee in her hands. "Come over here and have a seat, Janet, is it? We may be in for a long night."

Chapter 59

Inside, Janey felt a strange calm descend over her. She decided she would try and make some kind of connection with the drugged out thief. "My name is Janey, what 's your name?"

He looked at her with bleary eyes. "Don't make no difference what my name is," he said gruffly.

"Well, I just thought if we're going to be here for a while, we could chat to pass the time."

"Chat?" he said skeptically. "What are you up to?"

"Nothing, nothing, I swear. How about I tell you a little bit about myself and then you can decide if you want to share also...or not?"

"Go ahead, I ain't got nothing but time."

"Well, I have an identical twin sister named Janet and we just moved here about a month ago."

"No kidding...you look alike?"

"Yes, so much so that we use to fool our teachers sometimes."

That actually got a chuckle out of him. "I ain't never seen twins before," he said.

"Well, we have two brothers and two older sisters."

"Must have been nice, growing up in a big family like that, I had no-one, been on my own since I was 14."

Searching for more things to say, for more ways to connect, Janet replied, "Well yes, it was nice most of the time, but you sure didn't want to be the last one to the table!"

Laughing again, he said, "You know what, you're taking this really well. Most other girls would have been freaking out."

"Well, I was pretty scared at first. But I figure, whatever happens, happens. Crying won't change that fact. Do you believe in God, mister?"

"Name is Jake, and no, I don't. God never done nothin' for me."

"Well, it doesn't matter if you believe in God, Jake, as He believes in you. So if you ever get around to needing Him, He'll be there." Feeling uncomfortable, Jake turned away. She could see he was trying to control his jitters, but he was coming down fast from his high.

Suddenly, he started to cry. "I never meant for none of this to happen. I just needed money real bad, you know, because I'm so sick."

Janey did not know how to respond. "I don't know what I'm doing when I'm like this—I didn't mean to hurt no-one. That stuff I got this time must have been really bad." He looked like he was having a breakdown. His eyes were haunted as his wiped his nose on his dirty shirt.

Janey wondered what his story was that brought him to this place—at this time. What had transpired in his life to bring him to this crossroads in his life. He wasn't much older than her, and yet he had to have suffered severe trauma in his younger years.

Almost immediately, his demeanor changed. He grew angry and practically spit at her. "Don't think I'm going soft on you." He started shuffling back and forth, unable to stand still. His emotions were all over the place and that was what scared Janey the most. How could you reason with a space-out, violent drug addict? "Don't talk to me like you're my friend—you don't know me—you don't know nothing about me.

"What the hell is going on out there…where 's my money and my car? If I don't get it soon, I'll shoot the girl."

Janet dropped her coffee and jumped up. "Take it easy, miss, let us handle it." Manuel picked up the bullhorn and said, "We're working on it…takes time to get that kind of money so late at night. But I need something from you first. I need to see if the girl is alright or we stop right here and I'll just send in the SWAT team."

As Jake considered this latest development, he shuffled back and forth. The DT's were kicking in fast and he couldn't control his movements. He was sweating profusely and seemed close to passing out. Looking at Janey, he seemed to make a decision. He told her to go to the door and open it—stand there for one minute, then turn around and come back immediately. If she tried to run out, he would shoot her in the back. Janey believed every word he was saying and so she hesitantly walked towards the door.

Chapter 60

"That was quite a story, Kaleb." Noah had leaned forward to catch everything Kaleb was saying. Shane sat transfixed at their feet unwilling to move an inch. "But how did you get to this place in life?"

Kaleb smiled sadly and continued his story. He told of the many seasons he had returned to fish and how it was apparent that Ma and Pa were beginning to show their age.

"They began to embrace the end and spoke with me about their final wishes. They wanted me to have their boat, but I resisted at first as I felt I didn't deserve such a blessing. They were adamant saying that they had bequeathed a comfortable nest egg to you, Noah, and so wanted me to have the boat. They said that we were like their own children and that this final offering would let them die in peace."

Sadly, Noah interjected, "Yes, that money was so appreciated. It allowed me to go to medical school. I still miss them all the time. They were amazing people, I loved them both too."

Kaleb nodded and went on…"I continued to fish each season for the next few years, until my Mum passed and I was left to take care of the kids. I decided to sell the boats and start my delivery business. It allowed me to have a regular life on land where as I said before, I met Gracie."

"I'm so sorry you had to go through all of that, Kaleb."

"Thanks Noah…it was a very hard time for us…she suffered for so long. But I have never regretted that time for one minute because it brought me a love so deep—so transformative, that I will never again love another. We had a deep love and from that love came my son and daughter. My business has continued to grow and I am very comfortable now."

"Yes, I especially love your logo…maybe I should get a percentage?" Noah laughed. Laughing too, Kaleb said it reminded him of a special time in his life.

Chapter 61

As Janey opened the door, instantly it seemed a thousand flashbulbs went off. Turning around, she hurried back to the counter and Jake. She knew she had to keep him satisfied, hoping to get him off guard somehow. Jake motioned her back behind the counter.

"There she is…look, she's OK," someone yelled in the crowd.

Janet collapsed with relief. "My God," Manuel said in disbelief, "she's you!"

"I'm sorry, I guess in all this madness, I didn't tell you we were twins," Janet said wearily.

Suddenly, there were microphones shoved in her face, the many news outlets clambering for an interview. "How do you feel about your twin sister being held as a hostage?"

"Did you know this was happening by some psychic connection?"

"Will you feel half empty if she dies?"

Janet was speechless.

"OK, that's enough…get back, leave her alone. Will one of you officers get these vultures back behind the line?" Manuel shouted.

Manuel spoke into the bullhorn. "OK, thank you for confirming the girl is alright. Her sister is here, and I can tell you she was very relieved to see her. The money has been collected and should be here in just a few moments.

"Janet?" Janey gave a little sob. "Please Jake, you're getting the money. Please let me go now."

Jake looked at her and then looked down at his trembling hands. Where the hell had that gun come from? he wondered. What was going on? Who was this girl and why did she look so frightened?

Suddenly, he was back in time and standing in a dirty kitchen. Everywhere he looked there was filth. Bugs were scurrying all over the counters and the floor. He shivered and looked away. In the corner sat his mother, passed out and snoring. She was a big woman with long filthy hair. Dirty strands hung limply in her face and her body odor was overpowering.

Next to her on the table, was a multitude of drug paraphernalia. Flies were everywhere and he thought he might get sick.

His childhood had been horrendous. He couldn't remember a time when his mother hadn't be drunk or high…or both. As she didn't work (said she had a bad back) she had lots of 'friends' around to help pay the rent and get her drugs. Funny, he thought, her back seemed just fine whenever she was 'entertaining' her friends.

From a very young age, he had to fend for himself. Food was always scarce…but somehow his mother managed to get her favorite fast-food all of the time. He had dropped out of school very early…as it had been hell for him. He was viciously bullied by everyone…but that was not a surprise, as his clothes were torn and dirty and you could smell him coming.

He learned at a very young age to fight…and he did that very well. There were no rules, no expectations—no-one who cared where he was or what he did. He took his first drink at nine, his first pill at ten. By the time he was twelve years old he was a habitual drunk and addict—just like dear old mother. And like Mom, he got the money for his addictions any way he could.

He had learned very early on that his body was his commodity. He couldn't remember all the times he was forced to do unspeakable things—nor did he want to. He simply did what he had to, to survive. He had no friends—no-one who cared if he lived or died.

One day, after his mother had 'worked' off their rent, the man decided to come after him. This wasn't the first time some sicko had tried to get a little 'extra' on the side. But this time Jake had had enough. Grabbing a knife, he had no trouble fending the old drunk off. As he ran away, he never knew if he had actually killed him or not. It didn't matter to Jake either way.

Now looking around in confusion, blinking at all the flashing lights, he again wondered where he was. His scrawny body was shaking so hard you could almost hear his bones grinding together. He felt sick—really sick. Dropping the gun, he slumped to the floor. Immediately, he was surrounded by a small army of policemen. Manuel helped Janey outside for her reunion with Janet. As Janey looked back at Jake, looking lost and confused, she couldn't help feeling a little sorry for him. As they took him away, he looked at her incomprehensibly.

Chapter 62

"Well, I guess it's my turn to fill you in," Noah said. "The first few weeks, after you left I pretty much just rested up and gained more strength.

"After you guys went back to sea, I threw myself into my volunteering at the hospital. Around this time, one of the older nurses seemed to take a special interest in me. When I admitted I could not read or write, Rose was surprised and came into my room later and took my hand in hers and said, 'Noah dear, I've decided to help you learn to read and write. It will be my Christmas present to you.' 'But Rose,' I said, 'Where will you find the time with all the hours you put in here?' 'Don't you worry about that, lad, I have my lunches and breaks each day and as I live alone, I could easily come in on my days off!'

"Starting to protest, I was immediately stopped with Rose assuring me that it would be a pleasure to help a sweet boy like me. So began my tutoring. Rose was very patient and encouraging. I found it pretty easy really and it seemed in no time I was actually reading and writing. Rose said I had taken to it like a duck to water. I was shocked and excited at the same time.

"During that time, I continued to follow the nurses around and they began to give me more and more to do. Seeing my excitement and interest in all things technical, Rose had a talk with the doctor. One day, the doctor came to my room to chat with me.

Rose was determined to help young Noah. He had touched her heart with his smile and grit. The more time Rose spent with Noah the more she felt fulfilled. She had spent most of her life nursing and had always loved it. But never before had a patient become like family to her.

She didn't recognize that subconsciously, Noah reminded her of her little brother. That revelation would reveal itself soon. She lived a simple life and had never married. She really had no friends outside work. When not at the hospital she volunteered wherever was needed and was an avid reader. She spent time each day helping Noah to learn how to read and write. Working with him was such a pleasure. As he became more literate, she gave him more duties around the hospital. Checking charts and reading medicine labels—Noah thrived on it.

Chapter 63

When Rose had been 10 years old, she was told by her parents that she was going to be a big sister. She was so excited! Her parents who had given up of ever having another child were ecstatic as well. Rose's father was a mailman and her mom worked in an office. Their little family was over the moon waiting to see this child. It was an easy pregnancy and even easier delivery.

The nurses could not believe that the labor only lasted three hours. The mom laughingly told them "I'm not complaining!." The little baby was named Jesse and he was the most beautiful little boy. His parents doted on him and Rose loved Jesse too. They would play together with Rose pretending to be his mother for hours on end. Jesse was her real-life little doll. As Jesse grew (and he grew really fast), he charmed everyone.

Not only did he walk before his time, his ability to speak astounded them as well. His gift of gab was so cute and he made them laugh over his silly antics. He was Daddy's little shadow. Jesse followed him around everywhere. Mom would come in and find the two of them sitting side-by-side on the sofa. Jesse had squeezed in right beside his Daddy. While sitting there, Jesse would be unconsciously twirling a lock of his hair. What a beautiful sight to see.

Mom would give silent prayers every day to God for giving her their beautiful little family. Rose was a beauty as well. Long curly soft brown hair framed a pretty face and beautiful smile. She was an artist who could draw beautiful pictures, and she had learned how to play on their old piano by herself. Jesse would stand beside her while she played, his head barely able to see the keys.

Jesse's eating habits were legendary as well. By two years old, he was eating more than his big sister (although at times, Rose was a picky eater). Not so with Jesse. "More cheese please, more kobassa." He would eat everything you put on his plate, with corn-on-the-cob being his newest favorite. By the time Jesse would finish, his whole face, hands and t-shirt would be covered in butter and kernels. It was too funny.

Friends would comment that when he was a teenager, Jesse would eat them out of house and home. Jesse was so smart as well… His little brain worked overtime. One night, while Mom was getting him ready for bed, Jesse asked in his sweet little voice, "I seep 2 bedroom, Mommy?"

For a minute, she had to think what he meant, and then it became clear. Jesse wanted to sleep with them, and because Mommy and Daddy slept there— it was 2 bedroom. As he was barely 2 years old, his reasoning astounded her. She scooped Jesse up and hugging him said, "No honey…no two bedroom, you sleep in Jesse's room."

Then there was the day when his daddy had gone into the bathroom to shave. Of course, Jesse had followed and was waiting outside the door. He kept saying "Daddy, Daddy, Daddy". Thinking it would be funny, his face covered with shaving cream, Daddy yanked open the door, leaned down and said, "BOO".

Jesse was startled. He backed up and turned away yelling, "Bad Daddy…Bad Daddy!" It took some time for Daddy to convince Jesse it was just a joke. Daddy never did that again!

Christmas was a big deal at our house, Rose remembered. Mom started decorating at the beginning of November! She turned their house into a winter wonderland. The lights and decorations were legendary. They put up two big trees, each with their own theme. Mom would have preferred real trees, but there was no way she could wait till just before Christmas to put them up! Smaller trees also decorated other rooms. We had musical ornaments and winter scenes that moved to music. It truly was a sight to behold. Christmas carols were played and Christmas cards sent out by the dozens. The outside was not forgotten either, as it too was covered with festive lights and ornaments.

Mom started baking Christmas goodies early as well. Cookies and squares and cakes…it was never ending. The baking would last way into the New Year. And presents! Lord, there were mountains of them. Brightly colored paper and bows, in Christmas bags and in all shapes of boxes. Can you imagine what all this would look like to a two-year-old little boy? Jesse was beside himself with anticipation.

Jesse had a little play tent set up in the living room. He loved going inside to 'hide' from us. After explaining to Jesse for the 100th time that he could not open presents until Christmas Eve (now I realize how impossible that would have been for him), we all sat down for dinner.

Jesse was not at the table, but we saw his two big feet sticking out of his tent. Then we heard the sound of paper ripping and started to laugh. Jesse was smart enough (or maybe sneaky enough) to figure he could fool us all and open a present inside his tent. But he didn't count on his adorable big feet sticking out. The jig was up!

Chapter 64

It was a day like every other day. Daddy and Jesse had picked up Mommy at work. Jesse was happily chatting away in the back seat to no-one in particular. Dad had told Mom that he had put the casserole in the oven and that it should be ready when they got home. She smiled at him and once again, repeated a silent prayer thanking God for the gift of such a loving family.

When they arrived home, Jesse asked if he could play in the backyard. Since it would only be a few minutes until she had dinner on the table, Mom said, "OK honey." Several moments later, the table set, she called out to Jesse to come in. There was no reply. Again she called his name but heard only silence.

Immediately, her heart began to race, as she just knew something was wrong. Jesse always answered her…always. Panicking, she called up to Rose to see if Jesse was with her. Coming down the stairs, Rose said no, she hadn't seen him. Twirling around, with tears streaming down her face, she flung open the front door and cried to her husband, "There's something wrong…I can't find Jesse…Dear God…where is he?"

Jesse's Dad tried to soothe his wife. "Calm down, he's probably just playing hide-and-seek."

"No, no he would have answered me." By this time Mom was getting hysterical and Rose had started crying too.

"It's OK. I'll check the backyard, we'll find him." As they opened the patio doors, Mother scanned the backyard again. As the Dad walked around the above-ground pool, the mother screamed. "Oh my God, Oh my God…. the pool, the pool."

It wasn't a very big pool but everyone enjoyed it throughout the previous summer, and Jesse had just loved it. It still had the winter covering on it, as it had not been open for the season yet. It was only March 26 and the cover was smooth, seemingly untouched. But she just knew. "Pull it back...pull it back...hurry, hurry...Dear God!"

As she stood there at the edge, Rose behind her crying, her eyes were glued to the pool. It took several pulls by Dad on the ground to move the heavy tarp even slightly. Looking down, Mother screamed and jumped in. His little body was on the bottom, unmoving. Screaming and crying, Mom lifted him out to Dad's arms, unto the deck.

Jesse still had on one of his little red boots. "Blow in his mouth. Blow in his mouth!" Mom screamed almost incoherently. Frantically, she tried to get out of the pool to be with her son, but as they had not opened the pool yet for the season, there was no ladder to climb out. "Rose, call an ambulance," she sobbed, watching dad trying to perform CPR. She kept screaming, "Get me out... get me out!"

Finally, Rose threw a chair in the pool and Mom was able to climb out to her son. He was deathly pale and unmoving. Mom and Dad were sobbing as the ambulance men arrived. They didn't stop to ask questions, they just grabbed Jesse and ran to their vehicle.

Mom and Dad following in their car, Mom soaking wet and chanting, "Please God, Please God, Please God" all the way to the hospital.

When they arrived there, the nurses and Doctor were working on him feverishly. Mom and Dad stood by sobbing, frantic to see any response. Mom started rubbing Jesse's head and softly singing their favorite songs. Other families in the ER with less serious issues looked over in dismay and started to cry as well. They silently prayed for this little boy. He was only 2 1/2 years old...not long enough, Father...not nearly long enough. Dad stood helplessly behind. It was as if he were made of stone.

We were asked to wait in the waiting room, to allow the staff to work. At some point a nurse brought Mom a blanket but she just said...never mind about me...save my son. The nurse touched her shoulder and sadly walked away. That's when the bartering began in earnest. "Please God. Please save Jesse, I promise I will never eat another trench fry again if you save my little sweetheart."

That may have sounded strange to most people, but if you knew my Mother, you would've known that giving up trench fries was the biggest sacrifice she could think of. Mom could literally eat fries daily until she died. So to offer this up to Jesus was the biggest offering she could make. I'm sure Dad was making his own deal with God, as were we all. But we learned you couldn't make deals with God…you would have to learn to live with His decisions.

Chapter 65

After what seemed like hours, the doctor came out to speak with us. His face was filled with sorrow as he took Mom's hand. "I am so sorry," he began.

"No. No, don't say it…Dear God, don't say it."

The kindly doctor continued, "We tried everything to save this young fellow…we even continued CPR way past the recommended time…but it just wasn't meant to be. I'm so sorry," he said again as he walked away.

I was in shock, but Mom and Dad were devastated. The next few days ran together as one long endless agony. The pall over the house was thick and impenetrable. No words were spoken…there was nothing to say. Mom and Dad seemed to retreat into their own private pain, neither one talking to the other. I was more or less forgotten.

At first I felt hurt, as I thought, *Hey, what about me…I'm still here*. I would turn 13 just a couple of weeks later…and I did not yet understand the dynamics of the situation. As I matured, I realized that my parents hadn't stopped loving me…they just couldn't get past the enormity of their anguish.

As time went on, they were able to climb back out from their pits of despair. Things returned to some semblance of ordinary, as they tried really hard to focus on me and my unfolding life. But always, the underlining sadness was there. It was unrelenting.

Even Christmas was not the joy it once was. Mom and Dad tried really hard to recapture the magic, but even though everything was still done as before—the baking and decorating, it felt like they were just going through the motions. The light in our family had been snuffed out, and things were never really the same. With age came wisdom, and I realized how hard it must have been for them to celebrate, wholeheartedly, with one child, while forever mourning another.

Thinking back to that time, gave me much needed clarity. I now knew what had precipitated my desire to become a nurse. I wanted to be able to help others in need as I wasn't able to help sweet Jesse. Years passed and as I graduated and become a registered nurse, I witnessed countless situations similar to Jesse's. As I tried to comfort the families, I paid special attention to siblings. Trying to assure them that once their parents had worked through this tragedy, they would once again feel the full measure of their parents' love.

After my parents died, I was inconsolable. Feelings of regret and shame filled my consciousness as I remembered how I had treated my parents. I blamed them for everything, Jesse's accident, their inability to get over it fast enough, and finally, their lack of attention to me. I realized now that my feelings of abandonment came from a young child's perspective. Time and maturity allowed me to see the big picture, rather than just my little piece of it. When I thought back to the many times I was harsh and hurt them, the many times I refused their apologies…it broke my heart. They never gave up on me though and even at the end of their days, they forgave me and professed their love.

I threw myself into my work. When I wasn't working, I was volunteering. Only when I kept busy, could the ghosts of my past be silenced. I dated a little, but I never found anyone who could fill the void in my life besides nursing. Finally, I just stopped trying. I resigned myself to what I had chosen for my life. The love and connection missing in my private life was filled at work, with my patients. They gave me the attention I lacked and most importantly gave me the satisfaction of allowing me to help them recover, as I had not been able to help sweet Jesse.

Years passed, and I grew older (and hopefully wiser). I had a lovely apartment, was comfortably set financially, and almost never thought of past sorrows.

And so I now understood why Noah had touched me like no other. Although the age was off and the circumstances were different, something about this young boy reminded me of my little brother Jesse. His slight frame and almost angelic face brought me back subconsciously to another tragic little boy. This is why I inserted myself into all things Noah. I was bound to help save this sweet boy in remembrance of Jesse.

'Noah, I've been told that you have been a great help to my nurses and that you seem to have an affinity to this work and a special rapport with the patients."

"Yes Dr Stokes, I love to help out wherever I can."

"Is this something you would like to make your life's work, son?"

"Oh doctor, that would be a dream come true but I've just learned to read and write, I have no proper schooling."

"Well, Rose says you are the smartest boy she's ever met and if you can show me that you're willing to work hard…"

"But doctor…I have no money for medical school and no place to stay while in school!"

"Prove to me you are as good as the nurses think…and you can move in with me. I'm a widower and would love to have someone to talk to—not to mention my rather extensive medical library just waiting to be used. And when the time comes, the money will be there for medical school."

Chapter 66

Finally arriving home in the early morning, the sisters hugged each other tightly and fell into bed. There were decisions to be made, but they would wait until tomorrow. They both slept in till late afternoon, still exhausted from the ordeal the previous night. Of course, there was the lengthy phone call from their family (with Kaleb threatening to bring them home immediately).

As they talked, they both decided that working at the bodega had to stop. But what were they to do? they thought. Janet still had not found work and now Janey was quitting her job. They decided to go outside for some fresh air. As Janet put her coat on, she felt something in her pocket.

Pulling out the embossed card, they remembered the young man and his offer.

Chapter 67

Dr. Stokes was everyone's favorite doctor. If he had a white beard he could be mistaken for Santa Claus! He was kind of round and almost always jolly. He never rushed a patient, he would always take time to actually listen to them. This kind behavior certainly rubbed off on young Noah.

He admired Dr. Stokes and the way he cared for his patients. Dr. Stokes had been widowed for many years now. His young wife had died during childbirth and unfortunately, so did their child. He never remarried and always said "lightning never strikes twice" whenever someone would try and introduce him to some young girl. He'd always say, "I had the best—and you can't do better than that."

Over the years, Dr. Stokes and Rose came to rely greatly on each other. They both admired each other's ability and commitment to their job. Gradually their working relationship blossomed into a warm friendship. They would have dinner together occasionally...but always to discuss a patient. Even though many of their co-workers assumed they were becoming more than friends they never crossed that line. They both treasured their deep friendship too much to put that at risk. So when Rose spoke of Noah in such glowing terms, Dr. Stokes was impressed.

I couldn't believe my luck! I was in shock! Why was God blessing me like this? I prayed on it and decided that everything I had gone through had led me to this path. That was when the thirst for knowledge really grabbed hold of me. I started reading everything I could get my hands on, eventually graduating to medical journals.

And so started a three-year journey to get me ready for the entrance exam into pre-med school. Besides helping out at the hospital...my studies consumed me. I kept in touch with Ma and Pa and shared each goal accomplished on my path to become a doctor. They wrote back how proud of me they were and that they loved me very much.

Finally, I was ready to take the test. I was elated to find out that I was accepted into medical school, however the joy turned to sadness when I was informed that Ma and Pa had passed together in their sleep. They were found holding hands. I smiled a little knowing this was exactly how they would have wanted to go. A lawyer contacted me shortly after their funeral and handed me a thick brown envelope.

Inside was a note from them both, telling how much they had loved me and that I was the son they wished they had. It also contained enough money to pay for the 3 years of medical school. I was shocked but humbled. These dear people had given me so much.

Chapter 68

The next 3 years living with Dr Stokes while attending medical school were some of the happiest of my life. It was like having a live-in professor and I learned so much from him. We spent countless hours ruminating over a sherry in front of a roaring fire.

Again, I was blessed with yet another father figure. Not only was he a wealth of knowledge, but being alone for so long Dr. Stokes could add one more title to his name…Top Chef. His meals were delicious and I felt spoiled. We had a system at home…Dr. Stokes cooked and I cleaned up. I felt I had the better deal. Between my studies and my volunteering at the hospital I had little time for anything else. Not missing a social life, I was content with how things were going. How could I complain, I had a beautiful home to live in, a wonderful teacher/father figure and I was pursuing my dream. I was a very lucky man indeed.

The year before I graduated, Dr. Stokes fell ill. I noticed he was slowing down but assumed it was just his age. He started forgetting some things and began to repeat conversations as well, so I began to really worry about him. As he became more feeble, his walking became unsteady. Finally, he had to take to his bed and he went downhill fast.

On the last day, I sat by his bed holding his shaking hand and tried to give him strength. This wonderful man, this loving man who had such an illustrious career, who had helped so many others, was reduced to a pitiful shadow of himself. Holding back my tears, I told him how much he had changed my life and how much I loved and respected him.

In a moment of clarity, he looked into my brimming eyes and spoke so softly I had to lean down to hear him. "I was the lucky one, son, for you filled my last years with love and friendship. Always remember they are people first and patients second." As he breathed his last breath, I thanked God for this wonderful man and made a promise to always follow his rule.

"I was devastated not only for losing yet another loved one…but because he had played such a pivotal role in my becoming a doctor…I had so hoped he would be there to enjoy the moment with me. I went through a dark period then, Kaleb, I don't mind telling you. I had a crisis of Faith.

"I questioned a God that could take so many loved ones away. It just wasn't fair. Why did some people seem to glide through life untouched by pain or loss? Why did others seem to live magical lives, one good thing after another? After much soul searching I finally came to the conclusion that God wasn't simply going to give everyone a perfect life…in which case we all would still be in the Garden of Eden…but that He would give us solace and the strength we needed to get through any dark days ahead.

"I realized that there was a reason for everything that happens to us, but because we can only see our own little piece of the big picture…we would have to accept God's will and only at our passing, would everything be revealed.

"After the funeral, a tall, lanky gentlemen took me aside. He introduced himself as having been Dr. Stokes' lawyer and that he had been instructed to tell me that Dr. Stokes had left me his house and his entire inheritance…which was substantial. It would provide enough funds to finish graduate school and beyond.

"I settled into my lonely existence while I finished my graduate studies. Staying in the house that I had shared so many wonderful times with him, I felt closer to this amazing man. I still volunteered at the hospital and remained close with Rose. She was, by now, way past her retirement but wouldn't entertain the thought of it. 'Nonsense,' she'd say, 'the Good Lord can take me right here where I belong.' Sure enough, God saw fit to grant her wish and one day she was found, as if only asleep at her desk after her lunch break.

"The day came when I graduated, and as I walked across the stage to accept my diploma, there was no-one special sitting in the audience for me, but as I looked out across the auditorium, I felt all of the love from my loved ones radiating out to me. My Mum was there smiling proudly, Ma and Pa were standing and dabbing their eyes, and Dr. Stokes and Rose joined in."

Chapter 69

They both looked at each other. Could this really be the answer to their problems? As they debated back and forth on whether or not to call, the pros and the cons, they decided to just go for it. Couldn't be worse than what they'd just been through and at least they would be together to deal with whatever came their way.

Janet was voted the one to call, as she was the oldest (by 2 minutes) so as she dialed the number she had to admit she was still pretty skeptical. She was encouraged to hear a secretary announcing the company on the card. Happily, she felt it was on the up and up. When she explained how they came to have this card, the secretary put them through right away.

They were surprised to hear they weren't talking to the young man from the café, but with the CEO of the agency. He explained that they had met one of his talent scouts, had heard all about them, and was anxious to meet them. He then invited them to come in today at 3 pm. Hanging up, the sisters were ecstatic. "He sounds really nice, right?"

"Yes and meeting him at his office and not some bar or apartment sounds professional and safe."

"And the time is great too…not like if it had been at night." Giddy, they started going through their clothes. "We want to dress similar, after all that's what got us noticed."

"Yes, but not too matching—we want classy chic." They finally settled on similar dresses in complimentary shades and did their hair and make-up as they always did. Twirling around in front of their mirror as they were leaving, they knew they were definitely eye-catching. As they flagged down a cab, they had forgotten, in the moment, the drama of last night.

Chapter 70

"I made my way to New York City where I interned in various hospitals. The next couple of years were grueling…but so rewarding. The days were long and the nights even longer. Each day I learned something new and witnessing how a large hospital was run was truly amazing. There was so much to learn, at times it was overwhelming. A couple of the new interns dropped out as they found it too hard to continue.

"I, however, was adamant I would succeed. I told myself…this was it…I was placed on the earth to do this. Many of my colleagues shared my views and opinions concerning patient wellness and agreed that a better outcome was possible if their mental state was treated at the same time. But I must admit there were a few doctors in Pediatrics that really scared me.

"Their beliefs regarding who should be treated and who should not, if they were handicapped in some way, was horrifying to me. They felt it would only strain limited resources and take it away more deserving patients. They clearly believed they should only use their expertise on those children that would have the highest rate of survival.

"They called this ' bio-ethics' and this skewered way of thinking was actually being taught. I couldn't believe what I was hearing. These 'educated men' would not pass an injured animal on the side of the road without trying to help. How then could they turn a blind eye to children in pain—no matter what their circumstances?

"I reminded them of the *doctors creed* which stated 'they were bound to heal the *needy*—not the most deserving.' I felt this would be a slippery slope as to who would fit their criteria of deserving their time and knowledge. I was however unable to sway these 'forward thinkers', and so I had to simply continue with my learning.

"Then I was lucky enough to get my residence here. It was a dream come true. I loved learning new things constantly and most of all, I loved my patients.

Nothing gave me greater pleasure than healing someone and sending them back to their families. As I went through each day, I always remembered Dr. Stokes's final wish. I know it made me a better doctor.

"I decided to pursue infectious disease protocols, as so many patients had successful surgeries only to succumb to infection during recuperation. I just knew there had to be a better way.

"Because it had touched me personally as well, I devoted almost all my free time into studying how to better treat and contain infections. People started to notice my interest in this field and I was offered a fellowship to continue my studies. They offered me a generous salary, a well- equipped lab and I could still see patients on a regular basis. I couldn't refuse. After endless hours of trial and error, I developed a protocol, that if implemented completely, would reduce death from infection up to 85% and in some cases even higher."

"But Noah, did you not ever marry and settle down?" Kaleb asked.

Noah paused for a moment. "No I didn't. I was in love with the woman of my dreams. We met in post-graduate school and had one blissful year together. Katie and I had just gotten engaged, when an accident took her from me. She died from an infection that could have been prevented. I swore I would dedicate my life's work to trying to prevent needless deaths again. My work has always been my first priority and I don't see that changing anytime soon."

"Oh God Noah, I'm so sorry to hear that. It seems we've both experienced great love and great loss."

Chapter 71

"Well actually, Kaleb, I have another strange tale of lost love to tell you about."

"What do you mean, Noah?"

"On the day that Shane was admitted to hospital, there was another admission as well."

"Yes, by the sound of it, you guys had tons that day."

"Yes, but none like these two special cases—your son and an elderly man who seemed to have no family listed. He actually looked like he was indigent. There was something though that drew me to him. As I continued to keep an eye out for him, tests showed that he not only had the virus, but a blood infection as well. It was determined he would need a blood transfusion, if he would have any chance to beat the virus. When his blood came back, it showed he was 0-negative and we were all out."

"That must have been tough, man."

"I'm 0-negative, Kaleb," Noah told him.

"Don't tell me you actually gave your own blood to him, Noah?"

"Yes I did and I am so glad I did. He had slipped into a coma, but the transfusion helped him to regain consciousness. I was able to question him a little bit more to find out his back story. How could a man go through his life with no family or friends to speak of? He told me some things, Kaleb, that rocked my world."

"What do you mean, Noah?"

"He spoke of the one true love that he had lost…he told me how he had met this sweet young girl at a barn dance…at the end of crop season…of how he had foolishly left and when he returned to get her he was told by her parents that she had married and moved way. He said he never forgot her and thought of her almost every day of his life.

"He had met no-one who even came close to the love he had for her. Kaleb, he was my Dad…the person I never thought I would ever meet. There was no mistaking those blue eyes."

"Oh my God, Noah, how excited must you be? That was your Mum's fervent prayer that you two would meet one day!

"Congratulations old friend, I'm so happy for you. What is your real last name—that must have been amazing to find out."

"Finlay, my name is Noah Finlay," he said proudly.

"Are you going to keep in touch with him, maybe even let him stay with you?"

Sadly, Noah said, "Yes he'll be staying with me, but not how you would think." Then Noah went on to explain on how his dad had passed that very same night, and that he had arranged to have him cremated and would take him home where he belonged.

"Oh Noah, how horrible for you, to finally find him after all these years and then to have lost him again. You know I'm here for you always and our family will help fill your void. We both lost parents and loved ones through the years, but this must have hurt the most."

"Well, I have my memories and you have two living testaments to your love." Smiling sadly, they each marveled at how far they had come to get to this place of acceptance. Rather than waste time feeling sorry for what they had lost, they chose to focus on feeling grateful for the love they had found.

Chapter 72

Arriving right on time, the twins rode a beautiful glass elevator up to the 20th floor of the high rise office building. They had never been in such a glamorous place before and were in awe of their surroundings. When they stepped into the advertising offices, they were, for a moment, stunned.

The floors were black marble and the secretary's desk was white leather. The waiting areas boasted white leather furniture as well. The walls were white and had black and white photos of their many advertising campaigns. Looking up from her desk, the elegant woman smiled and said she would let Mr. Benson know they had arrived.

A moment later, a tall, young man came out to greet them. Extending his manicured hand he shook their hands. Following him into his office, they were taken aback. If they had thought the reception area was amazing…this room was unbelievable. The black marble floors carried through into the massive space. One entire wall was floor to ceiling glass, looking out over Central Park West. The other 3 walls were all covered in what looked like black silk.

The impressive desk was white leather. It had the illusion of floating over the marble floor. Two black silk chairs were positioned in front of the desk. The only other white in the room was a white onyx fireplace. You would think that it would be a dark, somber room, but the sun shone through the wall of glass, making the onyx fireplace sparkle. It truly took their breath away.

Mr. Benson wasn't hard to look at either. Black thick hair and green eyes, he looked the part of a top executive. His clothes were impeccable and his smile was dazzling. As he asked them questions, it was really had to pay attention. Janet seemed to be the most smitten with him, as Janey sat back amused. He asked them to call him Larry, as Mr. Benson was his father, he laughed. That explained the LB insignia on the fireplace that was so artfully placed it almost blended in with the marble.

"We work exclusively in commercials. Most of the better ones you've seen on TV were probably ours." he smiled. "We also do a lot of black and white photo shoots for magazines. I understand you have no experience in this, and therefore no portfolios to show me?"

Janet replied, almost apologetically, "No, we've never done anything like this before."

"Not to worry, just by looking at you both, I feel a professional photographer could take some stunning pics of you. Would you be willing to meet with her and have some proofs done for me?" Trying to hide their excitement, they agreed. "Fine, Lydia with take your information and set up a time for the show" As he stood up to say goodbye, he again shook their hands and told them he thought this would work out very well. Floating on cloud nine, the girls rode back down the glass elevator.

"Oh my God. Wasn't he amazing?" Janet sighed.

"Well I wouldn't kick him out of bed for eating crackers, but…" Janey laughed.

They spent the next 3 days until the photo shoot excitedly chattering back and forth. The photo shoot was scheduled for 7 am at the New York Zoo! What could they be selling at the zoo? they wondered. Who cares, they decided, just enjoy the experience. Tired but excited, the girls arrived at the zoo. They were met by an assistant and driven to the shoot in a golf cart.

Their senses were overloaded with the myriad of sights, and sounds and smells. Laughing and pointing out all the animals, they thoroughly enjoyed the 10-minute ride. As they exited the golf cart, they saw they had arrived at an indoor exhibit. They followed the assistant through the entry way and had to adjust their eyesight, as the cavernous space was dark compared to the full sun they had just left.

They still had some reservations about what type of shoot this would be. Would it be a professional experience or God forbid, something sleazy (as a Twofer in an X-rated movie, as Janet had laughingly suggested before).

They both shivered a little and then tried to cover their reaction with a nervous giggle.

A striking, older woman walked towards them, her hand outstretched. "Welcome, you must be Janet and Janey. Did I get the order right?" she laughed.

"Yes you did! I'm Janet and came first."

Smiling, Janey added, "Yes but by only 2 minutes." The woman told them that she would be the photographer on this shoot and to call her Lacey. She led them over to a long make-up table. There were several chairs and 2 girls waiting to get started. They had never seen so much make-up in their lives. And just behind the table there was a long row of costumes and accessories.

A younger girl (probably an intern) handed them a coffee. As they drank it, their nerves seemed to calm and they sat back and settled in to enjoy the day. It wasn't long before drowsiness overcame them. The last thing Janet remembered was that she wasn't feeling so good. *What was happening?* she wondered. This didn't feel right, and as she looked over at her sister, she saw that Janey was being carried out by some man. She was unconscious! *My God, what is happening?* she screamed in her head. And then darkness...they had gone down the rabbit hole...

Darkness...silence...no...wait...a faint sound of whimpering. Janey was trying to identify what was going on...trying to determine where she was and where Janet was...my God, was that Janet whimpering? "Janet," she whispered, "is that you?"

"Janey...my God, what's happening to us?"

"I don't know...last I remember I was feeling sleepy and then the lights went out. "

"This can't be happening to us...we checked them out...we were at their actual offices. How is this possible?"

"Shhh...I hear someone coming"

The door opened abruptly and it sounded like two men had entered, swiftly shutting the door. Within seconds, both of their eye coverings were ripped off forcibly, as both girls winced at the pain. As their eyes accustomed to the bright lighting, they looked around in disbelief. They were back in the office of Larry Benson. Slowly, Mr. Benson (Janet would never again think of his as 'Larry') walked around the bound twins, leaning in to 'inspect' their obvious charms.

"These two are to be treated special...no needles...no street drugs...they must be kept clean at all times. They will only wear the best designer clothes, shoes, and jewelry and be given the V.I.P. treatment, massages, facials...they will be groomed to be high-end courtesans...they will only travel by private jet and will service only the utmost discerning clientele."

"But if we can't drug them up...how do we make them comply?"

"You would be surprised at the designer drugs that can be tailored to the individual needs of each client. These new combinations will not only lower their aversion to ANYTHING the client wants…they will ensure that they actually feel they are participating WILLINGLY. This will be crucial, as there will be no fear of them trying to escape. These designer drugs will have them loving whatever is asked of them. That is why specialty acts such as these, if treated well, could last a long time and bring in massive revenues. Have them ready for transport by this evening."

Silent tears flowed down the sisters' faces. "Now, now, girls…we do not want any puffy eyes. Not good for business."

As they were forced to swallow some tea…Janet thought how wrong she'd been about this man. His smile was not dazzling—it was cold and calculating and those green eyes of his narrowed and squinted as he contemplated the income the twins would generate. It was all a front, she thought…the marble floors, the leather furniture. That money came from trafficking—not commercials. *God, help us please*, Janet whispered under her breath as she once again slipped into oblivion.

This time, when they woke up, they were strapped in Italian leather seats. The private jet was spectacular. Everything was done in shades of ivory with gold accents. If it had been under happier circumstances the sisters would have been ecstatic. This was how the other half lived! But their reality wasn't so bright.

"You're finally awake." They turned towards the voice that sounded familiar and saw that it was Lacey (the pretend photographer). "You two should feel very lucky…you have been chosen to join the ranks of a very elite few."

"There are many things we are feeling right now—but I can assure you, one of them is not lucky," Janey replied. Janet seemed unable to speak. Her eyes, however, were like saucers…and spoke volumes. "Where are you taking us…you can't just kidnap us—we are American citizens! We have rights."

Sneering, Lacey replied, "We can and we are, and where you two are going couldn't care less about the origin of your birth. From now on, the only 'rights' you will have, is the right to decide how you will deal with your new lives. If you're smart, you will go with the flow and enjoy all the perks that are coming your way. As for any lingering moral issues you might have—the drugs will take care of that. Just relax and enjoy the ride."

As she left the cabin, Janey grabbed hold of Janet's hand. It was cold and she saw her sister begin to shake. As tears began to fall, Janey's heart broke. "It's alright, honey…we'll get out of this somehow. We left a message for Kaleb and told him where we were going, so when we don't show, he will come looking. It's only a matter of time until we're rescued."

Janet seemed to quiet a little, but inwardly, Janey was not so confident. Even if Kaleb could track them down…how long would that take…and what would they have to deal with until then? Silently, she prayed for the strength to get through whatever horrors awaited them.

Chapter 73

Long after the kids had gone to bed, the two old friends sat comfortably watching the fire die down. Who knew all those years ago that they would end up here…as close as ever…as if no time had passed. "We both have come so far, Kaleb, from where we started. The Universe has taken us down such different paths—but here we are, together again! It was God's plan all along, wasn't it?" Noah asked thoughtfully.

"Yes, old friend, I truly believe that. It wasn't always easy…in fact, at times it was damn hard, but in the end we have ended up exactly as we always said we would be…best friends forever!"

"And you have just inherited a whole new extended family," Kaleb joked. "And I'm sure there will be plenty to keep Uncle Noah busy."

"I may have no children of my own, but I will be the best Uncle there ever was!"

"Laughing, Kaleb replied, "Be careful what you wish for, my friend!"

Smiling at each other, they realized how lucky they had been—how grateful for the many blessings they had received over the years. A feeling of contentment settled over them. Almost in unison, they turned towards each other and without any words, fiercely hugged, realizing this unexpected reunion was just one more blessing bestowed upon them.

CPSIA information can be obtained
at www.ICGtesting.com
Printed in the USA
BVHW031124090822
644144BV00012B/513